THE WOMAN'S BLOUSE HAD BEEN RIPPED AND HER SKIRT HAD BEEN TWISTED HALF AROUND HER WAIST.

"You boys try to force yourself on the woman?" Slocum asked in a low, deadly voice. "That's not too hospitable even for a place like Abilene."

Slocum saw the two men who had been inside the house go for their six-shooters. He moved faster than a striking rattler. The first shot caught one gunman in the hip, spinning him around, the second shot took off the other's hat, leaving him staring up at the sky in astonishment.

Trumble threw up his hands. A trickle of blood oozed down the right side of his face.

"You intend to get on your horses and ride out peacefully?" Slocum asked.

"We're riding out," said Trumble. "But you ain't seen the last of us. We got a right to this land and we're going to take it—one way or another."

"Next time you won't find the greeting anywhere near as cordial," Slocum said.

OTHER BOOKS BY JAKE LOGAN

JAKE LOGAN

SLOCUM AND THE ABILENE SWINDLE

BERKLEY BOOKS, NEW YORK

SLOCUM AND THE ABILENE SWINDLE

A Berkley Book/published by arrangement with
the author

PRINTING HISTORY
Berkley edition/August 1988

ISBN: 0-425-10984-4

A BERKLEY BOOK ® TM 757,375
Berkley Books are published by The Berkley Publishing Group
200 Madison Avenue, New York, N.Y. 10016.
The name "BERKLEY" and the "B" logo
are trademarks belonging to Berkley Publishing Corporation.

PRINTED IN THE UNITED STATES OF AMERICA

10 9 8 7 6 5 4 3 2 1

1

Every muscle and joint in his body ached, but John Slocum hardly noticed. The end of the three-month trail drive was in sight. He settled back in the saddle and peered across the hazy prairie toward Abilene. It wasn't visible yet, but he knew it was there. Every other cowboy in Frank McKenzie's company knew it too, and already tasted cheap, biting whiskey on the tongue and the warm arms of a willing woman around their necks.

"Slocum! Wait up!"

He reined back and looked over his shoulder to see McKenzie galloping over to him.

"What is it? Nothing to keep us from getting into town today, is there?" Slocum was as anxious as the rest of the company to spend his hard-earned money. The trail drive hadn't been as difficult as some he'd heard about—and been on—but the work had been difficult enough, and the sixty dollars pay would take a while to squander.

"Got a few strays trying to head back to Texas, but that ain't it, John." Frank McKenzie had seen too many drives. His hair had turned snow white years back, his gnarled hands snapped and cracked as he clutched at the reins, and pain, real pain, cut into his once-handsome features. Slocum guessed the drover was forty and looked seventy. The hard, long trail hadn't been kind to McKenzie, but he had proven to be a good man and one Slocum had taken quite a shine to in the past few months. He had worked for men a lot worse than Frank McKenzie.

"Word just came in from one of the outriders that we got a reception committee waiting for us."

McKenzie's tone told Slocum that whoever was going to greet them wasn't doing it with open arms. "They reckon our cows got Spanish fever?"

"Something like that. A bunch of do-gooders with their heads stuck up their asses, I figure. The townspeople couldn't care less about our troubles." McKenzie snorted. "Fact is, they'd welcome us if *we* had the fever instead of the cows. Towns like Abilene make too damned much money off drovers."

"Then it's got to be the sodbusters." Slocum heaved a deep sigh. It never changed. Every small town they passed by saw the huge herds from Texas as salvation—and every outlying farmer saw them as a curse destroying their fields and bringing disease to kill their pitiful few animals. Spanish fever was what the Texans called it. Texas fever was a more common name up north among the homesteaders, since they were sure it came off the Texas longhorns. Slocum had even heard an animal doctor call it splenic fever and claimed it came from ticks carried by the cattle.

Slocum wasn't too sure about that, but he knew this herd was disease free. What losses they'd had during the drive had been to broken legs from stepping into prairie dog burrows and from predators. Coyotes and wolves had been worse on this trip than he'd ever see. He reckoned this had something to do with the sparse rainfall during the winter of '74. The smaller animals had been hit hard. The spring of '75 had seen enough rainfall to bring up the grama grass and make the trip easier on the cattle, though most were on the scrawny side.

A few weeks in a fattening pen would get them ready for the trip to the Chicago slaughterhouses. But if the local farmers believed the herd carried Spanish fever, those pens would be closed to them. Skinny cows meant no sales. Worse, the railroad might refuse to transport.

Slocum saw his meager wages for the drive vanishing like a mirage in the desert. If McKenzie couldn't sell his beeves, he couldn't afford to pay his hired hands.

"Might not be that bad, Slocum," said McKenzie. "I got to ride ahead and talk with the folks. They got worries. Maybe I got a silver tongue to soothe their fears."

Slocum nodded. McKenzie had a way about him. Some drovers were hotheaded. Not Frank McKenzie. He kept cool and didn't even wear a pistol. Slocum shifted slightly in the saddle and felt the reassuring weight of his Colt Navy slung in the soft leather cross-draw holster. During the drive he hadn't worn it often, but he had been expecting to get into town. Even without a bunch of drunk cowboys to contend with, some cattle towns had their share of fools wanting to challenge anyone who rode in.

This had happened to Slocum too many times to remember. He didn't doubt that it would happen again, maybe in Abilene. He wanted to be ready for it.

"There won't be any gunplay, John," assured the drover. "Joe McCoy's dealt with trouble like this before. He's a good man. He won't let our beeves starve to death out here."

"No one makes any money from that," agreed Slocum. He ran a dirty hand through his lank, dark hair. Joseph

McCoy had worked wonders in Abilene convincing the citizens to put in fattening pens for cattle, quarantine for longhorns, getting a railhead established and making the cowboys feel at home in the overpriced saloons. Slocum guessed McCoy had prospered because of this vision.

"You want me to tend to business while you're in town palavering with them?" asked Slocum.

To his surprise, McKenzie said, "I'd like for you to be along. Back me up if things get too rough." He held out his twisted, gnarly hand. "Can't handle a six-gun like I used to."

"Think there's going to be trouble?"

McKenzie shrugged. "Can't rightly say, but it never hurts to take precautions. I'd feel a damned sight better with you along. Kelly or Bokemper can watch the longhorns as good as you."

"Let's get down to it, then," said Slocum, never one to waste time. They rode across the featureless prairie, each lost in thought. Slocum wanted to avoid gunplay if possible. He had killed too many men for little or no reason other than that they picked a fight with him. Also, he hated to draw unwanted attention to himself.

Posters still circulated with his likeness on them, posters for crimes he had and hadn't committed. Worst of the lot had to be the judge killing. Slocum turned cold inside as memories flooded back. Returning from the war, he had worked hard on the family farm in Calhoun, Georgia. His brother Robert had been killed at Gettysburg, and his parents had died soon after. He had been laid up for months recovering from wounds given him by his own side.

Slocum touched the spot on his belly where four small, round scars marked the bullet holes put in him by Bloody Bill Anderson and Quantrill for speaking up about the savagery during the Lawrenceville raid. They'd gut-shot him and left him for dead.

But the real trouble came back home when a carpetbagger judge had taken a fancy to the farm, wanting to turn it into a stud farm for Tennessee walkers.

No taxes had been paid, the judge claimed; he could confiscate the property. The Reconstruction judge and a hired gunman had ridden up, fat and sassy and confident of the outcome. John Slocum had ridden away from the farm at sundown, never looking back, two new graves on the ridge up by the springhouse.

The law never forgave judge killers, even if the judge was worthless and crooked and a damned carpetbagger.

"We got a welcoming committee waiting for us," said McKenzie. Slocum had already spotted the four men—and the way the sunlight shone off blued rifle barrels.

They dismounted and walked their horses slowly toward the four men. McKenzie called out, "Howdy. You gents lookin' for us?"

"If'n you're Frank McKenzie, you're the one we're after." McKenzie allowed that he was. The spokesman spat, wiped his mouth, and then said, "Then we got a message for you. Keep your damned longhorns out of Abilene. We don't want no Texas fever ravaging our cows."

Slocum watched in silence. The men shifted about nervously. None appeared comfortable holding their rifles. He guessed they used them for plinking at varmints rather than gunning down men. This confrontation worried at their insides like a festering canker.

"We're not looking for trouble," said McKenzie. "We heard tell that Mr. McCoy's got quarantine pens where we can keep the beeves until it's apparent we're not carrying the Spanish fever."

One man spat and said, "We call it Texas fever 'cuz that's where it comes from. You ain't gonna bring those cows within ten miles of Abilene. You just keep on moving."

"Where are we going to sell them?" asked McKenzie in a mild voice, but Slocum heard the hum of strain. The peaceable man was approaching the limit of his patience with these sodbusters.

"Take 'em to Ellsworth or Caldwell or—what's that new place called? Take 'em to Wichita. Just don't try bringing them into *our* town. We don't want no trouble, but if you bring it, we'll take care of it." He hefted his rifle significantly to show their determination.

"No need to get riled over this," spoke up Slocum. From the way McKenzie jerked around, Slocum knew the man had taken the words personally—as he was supposed to do. Slocum watched him cool down as he realized how close to real trouble he had been. "People getting shot and dying isn't the way to settle our dispute, is it? You got a marshal in town? We can talk to him about this."

"Him?" The sodbuster's spokesman spat again. "He's no good. For a nickel he'd let Satan himself into town."

"Looks as if we're getting some more company," observed Slocum. He pointed. All four men swung around to see where he pointed. He shook his head. He could have drawn and shot all four from their saddles if he had wanted.

The two newcomers had badges shining on their chests and rode with obvious authority and determination.

"Damnation," muttered a sodbuster. "We don't need them meddlin' in this."

The marshal and his Negro deputy skidded to a halt in the dusty soil so that they separated farmer from drover.

"What's going on here, Jed? I told you to tend to your growing and leave the law-enforcing to me."

"Marshal Lewis is a mite too conscientious for my liking," another sodbuster said, as if speaking to thin air.

"Damned right I am, Larkin. I'll run all four of your asses in for disturbin' the peace 'less you leave right now."

"You and Lem gonna arrest us?" asked Jed.

"Part of my job is keeping the streets clear. Lem arrests

swine all the time. You might just qualify, less'n you get on out of here."

Jed spat, wheeled his horse around, and spoke quietly to his friends. Without another word, they rode off in the direction of town. Marshal Lewis sagged slightly when he saw their backs. He turned to face the rest of his problem.

"You boys lookin' to get your beeves into town, I see. Jed and the others are concerned about Texas fever. Wiped out all the local cattle in the past couple years. Rain's been spotty. Crops ain't growin' right. Puts them real uptight."

"No need for them to take it out on us," said McKenzie. "Our longhorns are free of the fever."

"Might be clean, as you say. We seen some strange happenings, though. Months after a herd comes through there's an outbreak. Can't rightly figure how that's possible, but when your back's against the wall, you clutch at straws."

"Abilene's merchants are more in need of us than ever, then," said McKenzie. "Think of the business we'll bring to the town."

"Has been hard, these past couple years," allowed Lewis. "The newer towns have been takin' away our trade. Hell, even Dodge City is getting more than its fair share of the cattle trade now."

"My cowboys have developed a thirst three months old. Can't pay them till I find a buyer for my longhorns. Can't sell the longhorns if your townsfolk keep us out. Might have to go to—what was the place those yahoos said?"

"Ellsworth," said Slocum.

"That's the place. Ellsworth. Might see if their town wants to cater to our like."

"Don't go getting too hasty about this, now," said Lewis. "I got a say in this. I'm captain of police in Abilene and have duties to protect both the town and its visitors." He turned to his Negro deputy and said, "Lem, you go back and see if you can find Mr. McCoy. He was supposed to take care of this."

The deputy rode off in a cloud of dust.

"Good man, Lemuel Washington. Hard to find deputies, since the pay's so low." Marshal Lewis spat, took another chew off his plug, and turned his attention back to the problem at hand. "You fellows get your herd onto the flats over by Mud Creek and wait for Mr. McCoy to soothe the ruffled feathers in town. No need to raise a ruckus when everything's going to work out just fine."

"Much obliged, Marshal. Just don't keep us waiting too long. My boys have been talkin' about nothin' else but seein' your fine town for the last week or more."

"I'll attend to it. Just don't go riding in till you got permission. Can't rightly say what kind of reception you'd get, otherwise." With that, Abilene's captain of police rode slowly back to town.

"Reckon that's the best we're going to do today, Slocum."

"Want me to get the herd moving?"

"I'll tend to that chore. You find one or two outriders and round up the strays. The way the sodbusters talk, they might shoot them on sight and set fire to them."

Slocum nodded. Every scrawny straggler might put an extra fifteen or twenty dollars into McKenzie's pocket. If the beeves had to stay in quarantine too long, this might mean the difference between a profit or a loss for the long months on the trail and the even longer months raising the longhorns down on the ranch in Texas.

As McKenzie rode back to the herd, Slocum cut off at an angle. The outriders might already have rounded up the strays. Then again, they might be neglecting business anticipating cutting loose in Abilene. If he saw them, he'd set them onto the strays. Otherwise, Slocum figured he could handle the chore by himself.

The prairie stretched hot and flat and dusty. By noon,

Slocum's mouth felt like the inside of his boot. He dismounted and went to a muddy stream flowing at the bottom of a small ravine. He spat out the water. It tasted alkaline. He kept his horse from drinking. As dry as the animal was, it would drink until it bloated, then die from the water.

"Not yet," he said, patting the horse's neck. "You've been too good to me the past few months for me to let you drink this swill." With some difficulty, he pulled the horse away from the stream and led it up the gradual slope.

He heaved a sigh when he saw a dirty, shaggy-coated longhorn on the far side of the stream. Even though he couldn't read the brand from this distance, he knew it had to belong to McKenzie. They hadn't come across another drover heading for Abilene anywhere along the West Shawnee Trail. Most chose one of the newer cow towns, but Frank McKenzie was a man of habit and tradition. The first drives he had been on had ended in Abilene, so his herd had to be shipped from here too.

Slocum mounted and crossed the stream, cut upslope, and circled the steer. The longhorn's brand burned into the flank proclaimed it to belonged to the Swinging M ranch —Frank McKenzie's.

"Heyup!" Slocum called, pulling his lariat loose and using the free end to whip the balky longhorn into movement. The steer snorted wetly and peered up at him with red-rimmed, hate-filled eyes. The animal was stupid and vicious and would bring a full thirty dollars or more if they fattened it. Slocum wasn't about to let this much money walk away.

He had yet to collect his sixty dollars wages.

The longhorn began the slow trip back to the rest of the herd. Slocum kept a sharp eye out for other strays and spotted one less than ten minutes after finding the first. He changed direction slightly. Two longhorns were easier to herd than one. If he could find two or three more, he'd have little trouble getting them back to the main herd.

He rode slowly and found the second one pawing and snorting and acting as if it had been in combat. Slocum frowned when he saw the blood-red stains on the tips of the horns. It had hooked some poor creature and probably ripped it apart. The strong neck and savage horns could bring down damned near any animal found on the Kansas prairie.

Including a man.

Slocum stood in the stirrups and made a slow circuit of the plains. A small dust cloud in the distance showed a horse racing away.

"The horse wouldn't be running like that if it had been gutted," Slocum said out loud. A cold chill passed through him. Horses had riders. If the horse was unhurt, what of its rider?

He herded the two longhorns in the direction of the horse, his sharp eyes studying the dry ground. The dust had settled and blotted out any chance of tracking.

He didn't have to be an expert to find the rider. The soft moans of pain sounded even above the pawing and snuffling of the cattle.

Slocum dismounted and approached cautiously, fingers touching his ebony-handled Colt. From the way the man thrashed weakly, Slocum didn't think this was an ambush, but it never hurt to exercise caution.

He dropped to his knees when he saw the bloody mud under the man. The longhorn had hooked him in the belly and ripped open flesh, exposing long, stringy gray intestines.

"Who is it?" The man reached out toward Slocum with a shaking, bloody hand.

"Rest easy, mister," said Slocum. "You've been hurt real bad. Don't go aggravating it any more than you have to." The man's clothing betrayed him as a farmer, and not a very prosperous one, at that.

"I done my best. I tried to keep it all in me. How did I do? Can't feel anything."

"Quiet now." Slocum stood and stared down at the man. Somehow, he had gotten too close to the nasty-tempered longhorn. Maybe he had tried to chase it off. More likely, the sodbuster had tried to rustle the cow. Times had been hard in these parts.

From the severity of the wound, times would get much harder for the sodbuster. Slocum didn't see any way the farmer could live beyond sunset, if that long.

2

John Slocum shifted indecisively from foot to foot, trying to decide where his duty lay. Frank McKenzie had entrusted him with fetching any strays. He had found two, both prime steers that would bring good money at market. The way things were in Abilene, any single longhorn might mean the difference between profit or loss for the rancher.

On the other hand, he couldn't just abandon the slowly dying farmer. Slocum's experienced eye showed that there wasn't anything that could be done for the man. The sharp tip of a longhorn had gutted him good, ripping away his insides. Pink froth bubbled from the belly wound, showing one lung had been pierced, too. That he had lasted this long with such severe wounds was a miracle.

Slocum tried to make him comfortable.

The man's eyelids fluttered open. "My name's Benjamin Carson. Got a quarter section not far away."

13

"Rest easy, now. Don't go taxing yourself," said Slocum.

"I've got to get back. Got a sod hut for me and my wife." Carson turned his head to one side and spat ugly dark froth. Blood trickled from the corner of his mouth. "Not my wife, not yet. Not yet." He drifted away into unconsciousness.

Slocum made his decision. He couldn't let the man die alone on the prairie, no matter what foolishness had brought him to this deadly end. Moving him presented serious problems, though. Even getting the man to sit upright might kill him. Riding was out of the question.

"Does your wife have a buckboard?"

"Not my wife. Not yet. She's so lovely. Claire's beautiful. Don't know what she sees in a man like me."

"You got a farm. You're probably a good farmer, a good provider. Why shouldn't she go for a man like you?" Slocum wanted to make the man's final minutes as comfortable as possible.

"She's from back east. Got a real good education. Met her in St. Loo." Carson spat again.

"What direction is your farm? I'll see if I can't get a flatbed wagon so you can get back to her. She'll nurse you back to health." Slocum's tongue burned with the lie. Even during the war, when he had seen young men cut in half by minié balls and cannonade, he had seldom witnessed such a terrible wound.

"That way." Benjamin Carson lifted himself up enough to be sure of the direction. He lay back down, wheezing and gurgling deep in his throat. He clutched at his guts to keep them from spilling out.

Slocum took a deep breath, then set to work bandaging the man's midsection the best he could. Why he hadn't bled to death earlier was a mystery. Slocum had seen some men who refused to die, no matter what their injuries.

From what he had seen of Carson he wouldn't have thought the dirt farmer to be one of them.

Slocum shook his head. It went to show, you just never know about people. Some were a damned sight stronger and more determined than they had any right to be.

"I'll be back for you. Keep thinking about Claire." This was the best medicine he could give the man.

"Only fifteen, twenty minutes' ride." The man clutched his belly even harder and moved to his side. The ragged movement of his rib cage was the only indication that he still lived.

Slocum herded the two longhorns ahead of him. He didn't reckon Carson would be alive when he returned, and he wanted something to show for the day's work.

In less than fifteen minutes of slow walking, he espied a thin curl of white smoke drifting up from a stovepipe. Riding closer, he saw the sod hut that had been crudely cut from the prairie to furnish living quarters. A buckboard stood to one side of the yard, and a lathered horse danced within the confines of a corral.

He couldn't be sure, but he thought this might be the same horse that he had seen galloping riderless across the prairie. It had left its rider and returned home. What message had Carson's wife gotten from this?

Slocum steeled himself to tell a new widow how her husband had died.

He herded the longhorns to the corral and got them inside. At the same time, he led the horse out. With the steers as feisty as they were and the horse as nervous as a long-tailed cat in a rocking chair factory, there might be more blood and innards spilled. Slocum noted that the horse hadn't been tended to. He wondered what that meant as he tied its reins to the top corral rail.

Slipping the restraining thong off the hammer of his Colt, he walked slowly toward the sod hut's door.

"Anyone home?" he called. "Name's John Slocum. Anyone there?"

The door creaked once, then shot open. The muzzle of a double-barreled Damascus-wound shotgun poked out. Slocum started to draw, then checked himself. The woman holding the formidable weapon was pale and shaking, but he saw in a flash that she hadn't pulled back the hammers. He wasn't even sure from the way she held the shotgun that she could hit him, in spite of the wide angle of fire.

"What do you want?" She didn't quite stammer, but her voice damned near broke with strain. Her eyes were wide and bright blue, in sharp contrast to her creamy white skin and the raven's wing black hair pulled back into a severe bun. Slocum had seen more than his share of frontier women. This one was fresh from the big city—St. Louis, Benjamin Carson had said.

"You must be Claire," he said in a soothing voice.

"How did you know that? Who are you?" She brought the shotgun muzzle up so that he stared down both barrels. The dark-haired woman had yet to cock the weapon.

"I found your husband out on the prairie. He's in a mighty bad way."

"His horse came back without him a half hour back. There was blood on the stirrups and the horse's hooves. Wh-what happened to him? Did you kill him?"

"No, ma'am, I just found him. He'd been gored by one of the longhorns." Slocum indicated the two steers in the corral. "I was out rounding up strays. Your husband must have tangled with one and didn't know how cantankerous they can be."

"His died from splenic fever last year," she said, as if talking to herself. "He thought we needed another. Don't know why."

"Ma'am, are you all right? If you don't care that I'm saying it, you don't look to be in your right mind."

Slocum's hand jerked for his pistol when she thrust the

shotgun toward him, as if to poke him. She still hadn't cocked the scattergun. He wondered if he could kill a frightened woman if she tried to pull back those twin death hammers.

"Don't," she warned. "I don't want to hurt you. I . . . I just don't know what to do. Who'd you say you were?"

Slocum repeated his greeting. "Your husband is seriously hurt. I don't think he'll live too long out on the prairie. Let me fetch him in your buckboard. Even then . . ." Slocum shrugged to show that Benjamin Carson's prospects weren't good.

"He's not my husband. Not yet. Not really." She sagged against the sod wall and lowered the shotgun. Slocum moved slowly, then caught up the weapon and broke it open. She hadn't loaded it.

"I couldn't quite figure out what he was saying, ma'am."

"We're going to be married. The preacher is coming around this afternoon to marry us. He should be here anytime now. Can't imagine what's keeping him."

Slocum saw that the lovely woman was distraught. He took her gently by the arm and steered her back into the sod house. "Let's sit down for a few minutes and talk this over."

"Yes, of course. Mr. Slocum, wasn't it?"

The sod house's low ceiling forced Slocum to duck his head. His more than six foot frame wasn't built for living like this. He preferred a roof of stars over his head, not sod cut from the Kansas landscape.

He helped her to a simple wooden chair at the table. Claire settled into it, then seemed to collapse. She put her head on the table and sobs wracked her.

"I don't know why I ever let Benjamin talk me into coming to this godforsaken spot from St. Louis. I hate it out here. And now Benjamin's upped and died on me!"

"He wasn't dead when I left, ma'am. Let me use the

buckboard and I might be able to get him back here." Slocum didn't add, *In time for the preacher to say words over his grave.*

She looked up at him, her startlingly bright blue eyes awash with tears. "Why are you doing this? No one else has offered any help at all."

Slocum didn't want to say that he felt a small bit responsible. After all, it had been one of McKenzie's steers that had hooked the man. "We all do what we can out here."

"You're very kind. Yes, please. Take the buckboard and try to bring him back." She stiffened and wiped her eyes and nose on her sleeve. "He won't be alive when you get him back, will he?"

"Ma'am, he looks to be a tough man. And he *was* alive when I left him about twenty minutes back."

She motioned for him to be on his way. Slocum silently left, getting his horse out of its saddle and bridle and into the gear on the buckboard. The horse didn't want to return to the place where its owner had been savagely gored, but Slocum used the whip sparingly and well and got the balky animal moving. It had taken twenty to herd the longhorns to the sod hut. It took him only ten to return, using the cut-up sod from the steers' hooves as a guide.

To Slocum's immense surprise, Benjamin Carson was still alive.

"You back so soon, mister? Glad you are. Keep fading in and out. Sky goes dark on me like it's turning to night. But it ain't, I can tell. Can't be. Afternoon's my wedding."

"It's still early afternoon," Slocum said, getting Carson up and into the back of the buckboard. He marveled at the man's tenacity for life. It surely hadn't been the way he'd bandaged Carson that had saved the man's life this far.

"Did you tell Claire I was coming home?"

"She knows you're on the way. She's a real pretty woman. You're a lucky man."

"I am. She's strong, but this might bother her a mite."

Carson moaned in pain as the buckboard rocked and rattled across the prairie with the hot Kansas sun beating down on him. Before they pulled into the yard, the buckboard's wood flooring had become soaked with blood. The man bled quarts and still lived. Slocum was beginning to wonder if anything would kill him.

"The preacher man show up yet? I gotta marry Claire. I want to." The man's pinched, pain-wracked face showed no fear—only resignation. He knew he was going to die soon.

"He hadn't when I got this rig." Slocum reined in and controlled the nervously prancing horse, keeping it from dancing away from the door leading down into the sod house. He started to call out to the woman but didn't have to.

Her pale, drawn face shone in the sunlight penetrating into the depths of the house.

"Help me get him inside," Slocum said. At first, Claire backed away and looked as if she might be sick. Then she came up and out of the sod house, her face even paler and more pinched.

Carson reached out a bloody hand and touched her cheek. To her credit, she didn't flinch.

"You're so lovely. Don't grieve, Claire. We'll be married this afternoon. Everything's going to be fine. I promised, and Benjamin Carson never breaks his word, especially to a woman I love."

He coughed, and bloody spittle ran down his cheek. She almost bolted and ran. Slocum's strong hand prevented her.

"Help me." Together they heaved Carson out of the buckboard. Slocum wrestled the man down into the sod house and onto a rude bed. "Throw a blanket over him to keep him from getting the chills."

"No," she said in a choked voice. "He'll get blood on the blanket. Th-there's only the one."

Slocum ignored her protest and tossed the blanket over

the dying man. He stepped back and studied Carson. He was fading by slow inches.

"Thirsty," he moaned. "My mouth's so dry. Like a desert. Can I have a drink? Of the rainwater? It goes down so good."

"No," Claire said. "It'd kill him." Her eyes fixed on the throbbing mass of intestines until Slocum pulled the blanket over the man's belly and hid the wound.

"It's not a good thing, I know," Slocum said, "but in this case, I don't reckon it matters."

"He can't die."

"Quiet." Slocum got the dying man his drink. Carson faded off into a sleep more like a coma. His breathing was even more ragged than before, and he shivered constantly, as if with the ague. Slocum took Claire's arm and headed her outside.

"I don't want him to die," she said. "He was supposed to give me this huge farm. Hundreds of hired hands. Servants. That's what he promised. The liar! The lying son of a bitch!"

Slocum grabbed her and spun her around. She struggled weakly, then collapsed against him, sobbing bitterly.

"Why is he doing this to me?" she repeated over and over. Slocum said nothing, continuing to hold her until the panic and anger had momentarily fled. He knew how she felt. She had been betrayed by a man who wasn't supposed to die.

Slocum had shared these feelings. His brother had died needlessly during Pickett's Charge. A damnfool general had taken it into his head to be suicidal and had taken a company of good men with him. Slocum had seen it happening and had been unable to aid Robert. His hand brushed across his vest pocket where his brother's watch rode. This—and the memories—were all he had to remind him of a decent man.

"How'd you come to meet him?" Slocum asked, wanting to get the woman's mind onto other, more pleasant topics. It wouldn't be long before they had to bury her betrothed.

"He was in St. Louis trying to get together farming equipment. Th-this is all homestead land. We got a quarter section, and Benjamin was going to prove another quarter next year on a patch adjoining. He said we'd end up with a full section of land in a few years." She pointed across the prairie. It all looked the same to Slocum.

"He said you were from back east."

"My family moved to St. Louis when my father's hardware business in Michigan failed. We started over—and prospered. While not wealthy, we were well off." Claire dabbed at her eyes. Talking about her family and past settled her nerves.

"You must have some education. You don't talk like most folks around here."

She smiled crookedly. "I've been to Mrs. Marron's Finishing School for Young Ladies. Graduated with honors."

Slocum had never heard of the school, but Claire spoke as if everyone had. He nodded as if he approved of such a fine upbringing.

"I had been courting a young man my parents severely disapproved of," she said, her eyes turning foggy with the memory. "Billy was an apprentice riverboat pilot. My papa said the day of the paddle-wheelers was over and that Billy wouldn't amount to anything. Mama said he was nothing more than a sailor."

"You loved him?"

"I loved the idea of being free to roam," Claire said. "But Billy sailed for New Orleans and never even wrote. It had been almost six months since last I'd seen him when I met Benjamin."

"In your father's store?"

"Yes. Benjamin spoke so glowingly of Kansas and how the land was fertile. Stick a seed in and jump back, he said. The way that man talked!" Claire smiled almost shyly. "I loved his enthusiasm."

"He's a strong man. Never seen anyone hurt that bad and hang on. He might live, with a lot of nursing."

"You're just saying that, Mr. Slocum. I saw the wound. No one can live after sustaining such an injury." She shuddered. "How can you stand being around such vile creatures?" She stared into the corral where the two steers locked horns and twitched their thick necks in mock battle. Slocum hoped nothing came of this play. If they got to fighting, the flimsy corral would collapse quickly and he'd have to chase across the hot Kansas landscape after them.

A moment's pang hit him. He ought to get back to McKenzie and tell him what had happened. One look into the lovely, troubled woman's cornflower blue eyes convinced him he should stay a while longer. There wasn't much of anything he could do for her fiancé, but he might be able to keep her calmed down a mite.

"Papa wasn't happy with Benjamin. He never had any confidence in the very people he sold supplies to. Said they were all destined to remain dirt poor." She laughed, but the sound carried no humor with it. "I ran off. Imagine that? A proper young thing who had been graduated from Mrs. Marron's School running away to join the man she loved."

"Sounds romantic."

"Romantic, yes, and very, very foolish." She heaved a deep sigh. "I am without any money. The land isn't even mine. We had to homestead it before title passed over."

"That's true, but as long as you stay on it, you can keep it or even sell your rights to it. For what it's worth, he was right. This *is* rich farmland. The drought has just made it appear less worthy than it really is. With the railhead in

Abilene, you can get your crops to market in record time and get top dollar for them."

"I'm not any good at farming. I'm a city girl," Claire said. She eyed Slocum and asked, "What about you? You a farmer?"

Slocum laughed at her ignorance. "Been driving cattle for some time now. Reckon my farming days are past, though I did well at one time." He remembered the lush Georgia hills and the crops the Slocum family had brought in year after year, good rain and poor. He and his father had been the real farmers in the family. Robert had been the hunter, able to put meat on the table no matter how sparse the game got.

"So you don't know anything about wheat growing?"

"Some," he admitted, "but not enough to help you out. Besides, I'm worn out from herding the cattle up from Texas. All I want to do is go into town and find some relaxation."

"Drink and painted women, you mean." Claire's tone turned cold. "You're all alike. Mama was right."

Slocum wasn't up to arguing with her. He moved away and tried to guess how long it would take to get the strays back to the herd. He had no business staying when work waited for him.

"Wait, I meant nothing by that. I didn't mean to insult you. You . . . you're not like that. You couldn't be. You're too kind."

"I am like that," he said brutally. "You'd better go tend your man. He doesn't have much longer. You ought to make his last hours on earth as easy and pleasant as possible."

"Stay for dinner. Please. I don't know what to do for Benjamin. I've never seen anyone hurt so badly before. Please!"

Her plea went straight to Slocum's heart. He had in-

tended to ride back to the McKenzie herd, and he would—
after Benjamin Carson died and had received a proper burial.

With the dark-haired woman clinging to his arm, they
went back into the sod house to wait for death.

3

"I don't know where my manners are," the dark-haired woman said, coming from inside the sod house. She carried a glass of water. She thrust it at Slocum as if it were a peace offering. He didn't rightly know what she expected from him. He had been walking the perimeter of the yard looking for a likely spot to bury her husband.

He figured this was the least he could do for her.

"How's Mr. Carson?"

She shook her head. "No change, though the fever may be worse now. He's ranting now about getting married." She smiled wanly. "It looks to be the least I can do to make his passing easier."

Slocum snorted. A preacher was needed—but it would be to perform the burial services, not to give marriage vows.

"I don't remember telling you my name. I'm Claire Pelak."

"Wish we could have met under different circumstances, Miss Pelak."

"Please, call me Claire."

Slocum was startled at this familiarity. Her manner didn't seem to be one at ease with first names. Mrs. Marron's Finishing School hadn't successfully drummed it into her head that she must always be formal and stiff with strangers.

He sipped at the tepid water. It lacked the muddy or alkaline taste he'd found in the creek. For all its warmth, it tasted like the finest whiskey he'd ever drunk.

"I'm going to have to leave soon and get back to the herd," he said, finding that he didn't want to. Something about the woman's vulnerability appealed to him. It didn't hurt that Claire Pelak was a fine-looking, well-mannered lady, either.

"Wish you'd stay, Mr. Slocum. At least for a while longer. Until Benjamin . . ." Her words trailed off, and the stricken look came back to her haunted face.

"Where's this preacher man supposed to be? If he's coming in from Abilene, I might be able to speed him up a mite."

"Would you? Yes, Mr. Slocum—"

"John," he said, interrupting. If she wanted to be on a given-name basis, he wasn't going to argue the point with her.

"Thank you, John. This is mighty generous of you. The Reverend Baskin was due out around sundown. We were going to have the ceremony, he was going to stay the night, since his circuit called for him to be over at the Cameron place early tomorrow for a baptism—they have a new baby girl, you know—and then—"

Claire broke down. She buried her face in her hands and sobbed. The wracking shudders made her entire body look as if an earthquake was passing through. Slocum put his arm around her shoulders. Again she turned to him, her hot, wet tears dampening his dusty shirt.

"I'm sorry. I . . . I never had anything like this happen before. He's dying, and I can't do a thing about it!"

"This preacher Baskin. If I inquire after him in town, do you think I can find him?"

"He wasn't able to get out to our place any sooner because of a funeral." This set off another round of sobs and sniffing. "Someone in town. Th-they were burying him in the Abilene cemetery."

Slocum held her close, thinking hard. It struck him as odd that the preacher man wasn't coming out until sundown when he'd have to stay the night. Newlyweds deserved some small privacy on their wedding night, even if the young bucks did indulge in a bit of a shivaree. Seemed that the whole damned county was up and dying.

Except for the Camerons and their new daughter.

"Let me get the strays back to the herd—I got a job to do—then I'll ride on into town and find your preacher."

"Thank you, John. You've been more than kind already." Claire looked up at him, her blue eyes rimmed in tears. He saw clouds of emotion floating through those azure vistas that he didn't want to probe. Better to do as he had promised and be done with the woman and her nearly dead husband-to-be.

"I'll hurry," he heard himself saying. Slocum pushed away and got to his horse. The animal balked at having to carry weight again without the benefit of a good rubdown or decent feed or water or even much of a rest. Still, the horse had served him well along the long trail from Texas and wasn't going to stop now. Slocum got the two strays out of the corral and put Carson's horse inside. The animal needed tending as much as his own, but that could be done later.

After Benjamin Carson died.

He turned toward the southeast and got his two long-horns moving. Along the way back to the main herd, he found another stray. Frank McKenzie was happy to see him return with almost a hundred dollars in beef on the hoof that would otherwise have been lost.

"You've done a good day's work, John," the drover greeted him. "If'n I sell for a decent price, there'll be a bonus for you—for all the men. You've been damned loyal to me since we left Texas."

"Got to get back into town," Slocum said. He explained all that had happened. He saw McKenzie glancing toward the three longhorns, looking at their horns for bloody evidence of Carson's accident.

"What'n the hell was he doing on foot around one of those cantankerous beasts?" McKenzie blurted.

"Can't rightly say, but from what his widow said, he was trying to rustle the steer to replace one lost to Spanish fever last year."

"Damned rustler," grumbled McKenzie. "Reckon he got what he deserved." He spat and looked at Slocum. "You get on into town and find this preacher man, but I want you back here when you get the rustler planted in the ground. We got work to do."

"There's no call for me to stay around. I'm not hankering to become a sodbuster." Slocum's eyes swept across the flat Kansas prairie. "Not in these parts, at least." He couldn't keep down a pang of nostalgia as he remembered happier days back in Georgia. If it hadn't been for the thieving judge, he'd be settled on that hilltop and as happy as a kitten with a bowl of fresh cream.

"We'll be movin' the herd in real soon, John. You're going to be here," said McKenzie, making it more of a command than a request.

Slocum nodded curtly. He felt a duty toward a man he didn't even know, but seeing Carson's guts strung out from the longhorn's hooking meant he owed him something.

Even if it wasn't anything more than getting a pastor to say words over his grave.

He swung into the saddle and headed for Abilene. He was halfway there when he saw a small knot of men gathered beside the road. From the clink of glass and the loud voices, Slocum knew the men had been drinking. Looking around for a way to skirt the group showed him no way past. The Kansas plains were too flat for him to find a convenient ridge to ride behind.

"There's one of them sonsabitches!"

Slocum slipped the thong off the hammer of his Colt and rode forward slowly. To turn tail and run now was contrary to his nature. Even worse, he knew it would bring these vultures after him like flies to shit. The only way to avoid killing was to face up squarely and try to talk his way out of real trouble.

"Afternoon," Slocum said, not slowing as he rode. The hair on the back of his neck bristled as he rode past. He heard more than one hammer going back. He imagined trigger fingers tightening and heavy lead slugs ripping through his spine.

"Wait a minute, mister. You're one of them cow-punchers, ain't you?"

Slocum reined back but didn't turn to face his accuser. "I am," he said simply.

"We don't want your kind riding into our town. You might be carrying the sickness with you."

"Yeah!" spoke up another. "You might have been fucking your cows and caught the Texas fever."

Slocum knew the men only sought to rile him. Any provocation for gunning him down would do. They might not even need him to say a word. They'd drunk enough to give them Dutch courage. That made them nasty, but the need to vent their frustration over a year of drought and bad crops gave them the real reason for bushwhacking him.

"I'm looking for a preacher. Baskin is his name. Any of you gents know where I can find him?"

"What you lookin' for Reverend Baskin for, mister? You got business with him?"

"Funeral," Slocum replied. "Over at the Carson farm."

"Carson? He's that greenhorn what came in last year. He's over by the Cameron spread."

"That's the one," Slocum said. "He ran into a spot of trouble that put him in a bad way. Doesn't look as if he'll last till sundown."

"What's this to you, cowboy?"

Slocum still didn't turn to look at the men. He let one of them walk around until he stood in front of him. Slocum stared down at the drunk from his horse.

"I'm just being neighborly. Where's Reverend Baskin to be found?"

"Cemetery," the man said uneasily. "He had a funeral this morning. Nothing Doc Pendleton could do about it. Poor ole Crazy Sam got kicked in the head by his mule." The man laughed nervously. "That's the good thing about being a doctor. You can bury your mistakes."

Slocum simply stared, his cold green eyes boring into the man. The townsman wiped dried lips, took a quick pull from the whiskey bottle he held, and then looked back at his friends. "Reckon you'd better get on into town if'n you want to catch the reverend."

"Much obliged." Slocum let out a lungful of air as he rode off. He waited for the flurry of activity from behind that would signal them gunning him down. It never came. He heard more clanking of glass as the bottle passed around. By the time the six men took their fill, the bottle would be empty.

Slocum didn't care if they passed out and fried under the hot Kansas sun. Served them right.

He put his heels into the horse's flanks when he saw the

outskirts of Abilene. The sun would be setting in another hour or two, and he had a long ways to go to get Baskin out to the Carson farm. He was starting to regret having any part of this, yet duty carried him on. And more than a little bit of it was feeling sorry for a woman who had come all the way from St. Louis and who might not even end up a widow. No marriage, no widowhood for Claire Pelak.

Slocum hadn't gotten much past the outer frame buildings of Abilene when he saw a man in a black broadcloth swallowtail coat, tall stovepipe hat, and bushy muttonchop whiskers flecked with gray vigorously using a whip on a balky mule.

"You the preacher?" Slocum called.

"That I am, sir. Can you give me a hand with this truculent beast, sir? I cannot get it to move an inch."

The mule had pulled the small wagon out of town but had decided to stop for the day and graze. Whether it was the sun or the notion of finding some tasty grass for dinner that had caused the mule to protest any further effort, Slocum couldn't say. Then again, it might just have been the mule's nature.

Slocum patted his horse's neck and said softly, "I was saving this for you, old girl, but the need's greater elsewhere." He fumbled in his saddlebags and found the three lumps of sugar he had squirreled away weeks earlier as a treat for his mount. Dismounting, he went to the mule and grabbed one long, floppy ear.

"Listen good," he said sternly. "You keep pulling and you'll get another one of these." He held out a single lump of sugar for the mule. The animal sniffed at it, then tried to bite his hand. Slocum moved quick enough to avoid teeth marks in his flesh.

The mule made short work of the sugar and took a few steps toward him for more.

"Get'er moving, Reverend," said Slocum. "I think the lump of sugar is working."

"You are a sign from God, sir. Much obliged to you."

"You *are* heading for the Carson farm, aren't you?"

"You must be a heavenly messenger. How else could a complete stranger know my destination?" The preacher took off his tall silk hat and wiped sweat from his forehead with a dirty bandanna.

Slocum explained quickly all that had happened.

"You mean to say poor Benjamin is dying on this fine day that was supposed to mark the glad occasion of his nuptials?"

"Reckon so," said Slocum.

The preacher shook his head. "Poor, benighted Benjamin. If ever a man was beset by the trials of Job, truly it is he. Nothing has gone well for him since he homesteaded. I was surprised—and pleasantly so, I might add—when he told me he had brought back a bride from St. Loo."

"You sayin' Mr. Carson's luck hasn't run too good?"

"No, it hasn't. What could go wrong, has. I felt a tad sorry for him, I did. Not a Christian pity, either. Just a plain human sorrow that nothing worked for him."

"His bad luck's holding. By the time we get there, it'll be for his funeral."

"Have you met the intended Mrs. Carson?"

Slocum allowed that he had.

"Benjamin spoke well of her, but I've never had the pleasure. Is she likely to need, uh, comforting after this great sorrow descends on her shoulders?"

"Seems strong enough to bear up," said Slocum, not sure what Reverend Baskin was after.

"I see, yes, I truly see." The way the preacher said it set Slocum's teeth on edge. They rode the rest of the way to the Carson farm in silence.

When Slocum saw Claire Pelak coming out of the sod

house, he was sure it was to tell him that Benjamin had died.

She startled him when she said, "He's conscious again. Has been for almost an hour. He's been asking where you were, Reverend. I'm glad you made it."

Baskin shot a sharp look at Slocum. "I was told dear Benjamin had perished and that this was a mission to save his immortal soul."

"He . . . he's still alive." Claire closed her eyes and swayed. "He still wants to get married."

Slocum dismounted and saw to the preacher's rig. The large mule pulled back loose pink lips and showed strong white teeth, asking for its reward. Slocum had to smile.

"You done good," he said, grabbing an ear to keep the mule from biting him. He held out another lump of sugar. The mule's rough tongue flicked once and the sugar vanished. Slocum then went to his horse, who stood by as if accusing him of desertion. He gave her the last lump of sugar, apologizing as he did so.

"It was for a good cause. Believe me, it was." The chestnut horse looked unconvinced but was happy enough with the single lump of sugar not to protest too much.

Slocum went into the house and took a few seconds for his eyes to adjust to the dim light inside. He went down the steps and stood just inside the door. Reverend Baskin knelt beside Carson's bed, hand on the man's feverish forehead.

Claire stood to one side, her face whiter than flour and her hands shaking so hard she couldn't control it. She tried thrusting her hands under her apron, but this only made it more apparent how agitated she was.

"This is very unusual," said Baskin, "But a dy—" He cleared his throat as he cut off the word. "But such a request must be honored. Please come over here, my dear."

Slocum saw Claire jump as the reverend put his hand on her rump to guide her nearer the bed.

"Brother Benjamin has requested that I perform the wedding now. Are there any objections?" Baskin looked at Slocum rather than at Claire.

"No," the woman said in a small, choked voice that made her sound like a trapped animal whimpering to escape.

"So be it."

Slocum found himself dragooned into acting as witness for the ceremony. He hardly heard the words as Reverend Baskin recited the ceremony. His eyes never left Claire Pelak. She was marrying a dead man and knew it. Slocum's heart went out to her, but he said nothing, even when the preacher asked if any among the gathered had objections to the marriage.

"Seeing's how there aren't any objections, I now pronounce you man and wife. You can kiss the bride."

Claire bent and lightly brushed her lips across her new husband's. Carson stirred, his eyes open and on Claire. Those dying lips tried to form words and failed. He sagged back to the bed, all life gone from his tortured body.

Reverend Baskin sighed and pulled the single chair over and sank down onto it. In the silence that had descended, the only sound came from the chair legs creaking under the man's weight. Baskin flipped through the pages of his Bible, moved a bookmark, and motioned to Slocum.

"No need to keep him here any longer. Let's get him outside where we can perform a proper burial ceremony. You got a spot all picked out for the grave?"

Claire sobbed, then bit it back. Her eyes remained dry as she helped Slocum carry her head husband outside and lay him on the ground. She pointed to a shovel leaning against the house.

"I brought it around. Thought to use it myself but couldn't find the strength." Slocum took the shovel and hiked a ways toward the setting sun and began to dig.

Within twenty minutes he had a grave dug in the hard prairie. Within thirty Reverend Baskin was saying the prayer for the dead. In forty, he was on his way to the Cameron farm, declining to stay the night after seeing the coldness in Slocum's face.

—

4

Slocum stood to one side and watched the woman. She simply stared at the mound of raw dirt, hands clenched behind her back and her head bowed. The wind began to kick up, bringing small streamers of grit from across the prairie. Slocum looked around and grew restive. The shadows lay long on the ground, and the bright red ball of the sun worked its way down over the horizon.

Left on her own, Claire Carson might stand at the grave site all night long. He went to her and said softly, "About time to get inside, don't you think?"

She looked up, her eyes dull. She nodded, a strand of midnight-dark hair falling across her face. The woman never noticed. Slocum took her arm and guided her from her husband's grave.

He couldn't help but reflect on how cruel life could be. Not married five minutes and already a widow. Benjamin

Carson's death hadn't been an easy one, but he had died happy enough. Slocum couldn't think of any other way to go.

"Got chores to do. Always something to do around here." She laughed without humor. "Should sweep up inside, but the floor's dirt. Not like it was back home."

"I'll see to the animals. You got any more than the horse in the corral?"

"Some chickens, a few tiny, half-starved pigs out there, and useless it's run off, there ought to be a mule for the plow staked around here somewhere." Claire made vague pointing motions showing she didn't know where the mule might be.

"I'll see to it. You go fix some supper and get the house cleaned up a mite."

Slocum worked in silence, thinking hard. McKenzie had told him to come straight back to the company after burying Carson. It sounded easy, and Slocum had intended to do so. But he couldn't just up and leave Claire Carson. Widowed on her wedding day was bad enough, but watching her husband die by inches all afternoon in such a bloody fashion had to work on her mind. If there had been family or friends to aid her, Slocum wouldn't have thought twice about leaving.

He wished Reverend Baskin had stayed, even if the preacher had more on his mind than salvation. Slocum had seen that much every time Baskin had touched Claire. Slocum couldn't fault the preacher none. Claire was a pretty woman and one too fine to waste away out on the prairie.

He brushed both horses, curried them, and found some grain for the dozen hungry-looking chickens. The squawking fowls tried pecking at him. He kicked a few away and won a measure of respect, except from the rooster. Slocum knew that he'd have to wring the bird's neck before it would cease its aggressive ways and didn't much mind. The pigs were quickly slopped, and of the mule he found no trace. It might have pulled free from the stake or some-one might have stolen it.

Reverend Baskin came immediately to mind. A pair of mules pulling his battered wagon would get him around his circuit faster than just one. Slocum shrugged off this possible theft by the man. Let the good preacher take the mule as payment for services rendered. He had performed two ceremonies in one day for the Carson family.

Slocum walked slowly back to the sod house, wondering what he was going to say to Claire. He had a job to do with the herd. Somebody had to ride the range to keep the cattle together. Being this close to a big town made the open-range-reared longhorns uneasy. They tried to get away from the main herd and often provoked fights that left one or more of the beeves unsalable from injuries. Slocum had shot more than his share of damaged cows ripped apart by the long, deadly horns.

The eating was always good for a few days after, but the owner complained bitterly about lost revenues.

He went down the steps and ducked, entering the sod house. His nose wrinkled. "Something surely does smell good," he said. Claire worked at a black iron kettle of beans and had already flopped some sowbelly onto a battered tin plate.

"Help yourself. I don't much feel like eating."

Slocum ate hungrily. Even with a cook along on the drive, he seldom had a chance to eat regular meals. Something always managed to pull him away from food. If it wasn't a stray, then it was the threat of a stampede or just simple tiredness. Although Claire wasn't the best cook in the world, he wasn't lying much when he complimented her.

"You're just saying that," she said, but she seemed genuinely pleased that he had bothered to say anything at all. An uncomfortable silence fell. Slocum never knew how to talk with people who had experienced great loss. During the war he had seen brothers killed next to brothers. A father had been blown apart in front of his son. Worst of all were the atrocities performed by Quantrill in the name of the Confederacy. Mothers were hacked apart as their children watched—and always Slocum wanted to say the right words to make the hurt go away.

Sometimes there weren't any words. This was one of those times.

"You have to be getting back to your herd, I reckon," Claire said. She sat on the edge of the bed, her hands folded in her lap. The woman's tone was level, almost calm. Underneath the facade Slocum felt the intense emotions raging.

"You got any whiskey?" he asked suddenly.

"What? Oh, yes, somewhere. Benjamin took a sip once in a while." She rummaged through a small chest at the foot of the bed and came out with a half-empty bottle of Billy Taylor's. She held it up, as if not knowing what to do with it.

Slocum took the bottle and poured a generous amount into a tin cup. He passed it to her. Claire looked horrified at the idea of demon liquor and started to refuse. "Go on," he urged. "A few sips of that will make you feel better."

"No, it won't," she answered, "but it might make me numb. That'd be as good as anything I could do right now." She lifted the cup to her lips, both hands clutching the cup.

She made a face as the sharp, biting tang of the whiskey hit her. She took another drink, longer and without choking. Slocum pushed across a glass of the tepid water that had accompanied his plate of beans and sowbelly. She mixed the water with the straight bourbon. This seemed even more to her liking.

"Do I have to drink the entire bottle to go numb all over?" she asked.

"As much as you want. It helps. I know."

"You've been around, haven't you, Mr. Slocum? I can sense it."

"Seen a fair amount of the West. Never been much for travelin' back east." He didn't tell her he came from Georgia and some of his earliest memories were of seeing the Atlantic Ocean for the first time. His father had taken him on a short trip to pick up seed ordered from England. Not only had he seen the limitless ocean but he had also seen the trading ships in Savannah harbor.

"We moved around. I don't remember much of it, but my mama told stories of the places we'd been and the things we'd seen." Claire took another stiff drink of the water-cut whiskey. "She might have been lying. Mama always was a storyteller."

Again silence fell. Slocum's green eyes fixed on Claire's bright blue ones. They seemed to grow bigger, wider, deeper. He felt himself being pulled down into her very soul.

"I need you, John." She said in her tiny, almost inaudible voice. "This has been one hell of a day, and I need you."

"It's not right, Claire."

"What's right? What's wrong? I thought I knew. I don't now. Is it right for Benjamin to be taken from me like this, before we were married for real?" She blushed, color coming to her cheeks. In a voice even lower, she said, "He never did more than kiss me. Said there'd be plenty of time after we were married. He was an honest, honorable, God-fearing man. Damn him for that!"

Slocum moved to sit beside her on the bed, knowing what would happen. He put his index finger under her chin and lifted the troubled face so that he stared directly at her. For a moment, the world hung suspended. Every small sound was magnified. He heard cicadas chirping. The horses in the corral nickered and whinnied. The pig squealed in the distance, and the wind blew mournfully, as if paying tribute to the dead.

But something was born between them. Slocum kissed her gently. Her lips quivered, and Claire almost pulled away. Then she threw herself into the kiss with a startling passion that took his breath away.

"I need you, John. I need you as a man. Give me what Benjamin never did. Please, please!"

His hands stroked along the lines of her jaw, moved around her neck, held her head. He laced his fingers through her dark hair and pulled her down more firmly. Their lips crushed with passion. To his surprise, he felt her pointed pink tongue forcing its way between his lips. Their tongues collided and danced back and forth.

She began panting with desire. She slid closer to him, her breasts thrusting against his chest. Moving slightly she began rubbing against him. Their clothing got in the way. Slocum began working to do something about this.

"Do you want to keep on?" he asked. His heart pounded, and the blood throbbed in his temples like surf against a shoreline.

"Yes!"

She almost ripped off his leather vest and shirt. With nimble fingers, she worked open the buttons on his long-johns and peeled back the sweat-soaked woolens until he was naked to the waist.

Claire licked and kissed him, moving from his lips to his throat and working down. Slocum liked the feel of her impassioned mouth on his chest. Her sharp teeth nipped, and her tongue laved. He sighed and leaned back. She followed him like a snake slithering up a tree trunk.

"I need you so much, John. Don't deny me. Don't!"

"No, Claire, I won't," he said, damning himself for a fool even as he spoke. This was no time to get involved with her. The woman's husband had just died. Still, in the back of his mind, he couldn't get away from the notion that she truly needed him—and his lovemaking.

His hands slipped free of her raven-dark hair and worked under the collar of her blouse. One by one he opened the buttons until he had her unfettered by the garment. He threw the blouse aside as she worked to get free of her undergarments.

He swallowed hard when he saw her naked breasts. In the dim flickering yellow light cast by the coal oil lamp, those twin mounds of succulent flesh took on a life of their own. They bobbed and danced, and the hard red nipple atop each one appeared to be a finger pointing at him—and beckoning him closer.

Burying his face between those snowy white hills, he licked and kissed and worked his way up the left slope. As he pulled the nipple into his mouth, he felt the throbbing of her heart beneath.

"Don't stop. Don't. I want more. I want what Benjamin never gave me. You're the one who can do it, John. I want you to do it all to me!"

Slocum couldn't have stopped even if she had wanted him to. The sight and taste of those breasts drove him wild. He pulled her closer, trying to engulf each breast in turn. His hands struggled with the fasteners on her skirt. He popped one button and pulled the eyelets and hooks out of the fabric in his haste.

Claire rose. He skinned off the skirt as she kicked free of the remainder of her undergarments. For a moment she stood naked, silhouetted by the pale lamplight. Slocum wasn't sure he had ever seen a more beautiful sight in his life. Her high firm breasts quivered slightly every time she took a breath. Her waist was wasp-thin, and her hips flared out enticingly. The dark patch between her legs called to him.

He reached out and touched the fleecy triangle. She

gasped as his fingers worked along the pink creases and found moisture already welling from inside.

"That feels soooo good," she sighed. She stepped closer, her legs parting in complete sexual abandon. Bending over, she got his gunbelt off and tugged at his denims. Slocum finished the chore by climbing out of his long-johns.

She stared at his crotch and the pillar growing there. Claire licked her lips and reached out hesitantly.

"Go on. Touch it. Take it," he said, realizing she didn't really know what to do. The thought that this lovely woman might be a virgin made his manhood jerk hard and stiff. His strong hand on her wrist kept her from drawing away as he began to respond to her touch—and the notion of what was being offered so freely.

"I don't know what to do. I've heard. I mean, girls talk, and I've seen the animals, but I've never . . ."

He cut off her indecision with a kiss. Pulling her down, they lay together on the small bed. Slocum forced away the memory of her husband dying on this same bed. He and Claire were together. That was all that mattered.

She needed him—and he needed her.

He rolled on top and gently parted her legs. Holding back was something of a problem for him. The tightness in his loins turned almost painful. It had been too long since he'd had a woman, yet he knew he couldn't rush. To do so might hurt her.

"Wh-what are you doing? Oh," she said. *"Oh!"*

He slipped forward, the head of his meaty shaft parting her nether lips and touching virgin territory. For a brief instant, he thought he had hurt her. The woman's entire body shook like a leaf caught in a high wind.

"I never thought. Oh, John. More. Give me more!" She clutched at him fiercely, pulling him down on top of her. "Make me forget everything. Make me forget!"

He slipped into her heated sheath slowly, taking his

time, making certain he wasn't giving her any pain. He didn't find any maidenhead, but that didn't surprise him. She might still be a virgin. Riding, even in a buckboard, twisted womenfolk up inside, he knew.

When he was buried to the hilt in her softly yielding interior, he paused and gazed down into her bright blue eyes. She stared at him without seeing. Her cheeks were rosy and flushed, and she might have been suffering from a fever.

But no fever had ever possessed a woman and given so much pleasure. She made tiny cooing noises. He kissed her, then began slipping free. She gasped and moaned, words all jumbled in her throat.

Slocum kept on with the slow fucking for as long as he could, but nature worked on him. It had been too long, and Claire was too pretty. His hips began to jerk and stab in and out. He fell into the ages-old rhythm as the heat built up along his shaft.

She sobbed and clutched at him just as he lost control. The hot tides rose within and flooded into her clutching, clinging interior.

He sagged against her, sweaty and spent. Claire moved from under him, but her arms circled his neck and held him close. She buried her face in his shoulder and, within minutes, was softly snoring.

Slocum stared at her. He had taken away her misery—for the moment. What was he going to do come morning? He pushed the thought away and drifted off to peaceful sleep with the woman in his arms.

5

Slocum woke when the circulation in his arm was cut off by Claire's head. She snuggled closer, her head pressing down into his arm. Moving carefully to avoid waking her, he got out of the small bed and stretched. His hands hit the sod roof and brought down a feeble cascade of dirt. He wiped it from his hands and off his shoulders before fumbling around for his clothes. During the night the oil lamp had burned out.

Taking the lamp outside, he examined it. Coal oil still sloshed in the glass reservoir. Slocum pulled out the thick-bladed knife he always carried and trimmed the wick. Using a lucifer, he lighted it and watched the lamp sputter and then burn with its usual clean, yellow light. He blew out the lamp and carried it back inside. There were always more chores to do than time to do them.

Claire slept peacefully. No sign of the horror that had

visited her the day before marred her beauty. She might have been a princess from a fairy tale curled up quietly on the bed. Slocum resisted the urge to kiss her. That might wake her.

He again left the sod house and went to tend the animals. Even on a pitiful farm like this one, chores had to be done. Chickens didn't understand when they weren't given corn, and horses tended to turn as balky as a mule if not looked after properly. By the time Slocum returned to the house, Claire was up and fixing breakfast.

"It's not much," she said. "The chickens aren't laying well. There's only a couple of eggs, but you can have them."

"I've got to get back to the company. Mr. McKenzie will be thinking some of the townsfolk bushwhacked me."

"They're not too hospitable, are they?" Claire pushed back a strand of hair falling over her forehead. "They never made me feel at home, and they downright snubbed Benjamin." The mention of her dead husband caused a moment's cloud of sorrow to pass across her lovely face. Then it vanished, as if it had never existed. "Got a passel of work to do. Reckon you do too, John."

"Are you going to be all right?"

"I'll get by. Don't know how I can possibly do everything that needs doing." She sat in the single chair, hands folded in her lap. She looked the very picture of dejection. "Benjamin only had a year's proving in on the farm. The homesteading law says we need seven for it to be ours. The way I'm feeling now, it might as well be a hundred."

"Are you going back to St. Louis?"

"Don't know what good that would do me. My family's there, true, but they well nigh disowned me when I ran off with Benjamin. Papa called him a no-account." She laughed without any humor. "Wasn't like that at first. Only when Benjamin declared his feelings for me did Papa turn against him so strongly."

"Eat your breakfast," said Slocum. "Eggs are scarce, but you'll have enough to get you by for a while."

"John?" She turned, her face lighting up with hope. "Will you come see me? After you've finished your business in Abilene?"

"Can't promise, Claire. Mr. McKenzie might want to drive the herd on to Ellsworth or even Wichita if they insist on a long quarantine here."

"I understand."

Slocum saw her shoulders slump. She *did* understand. He settled his hat on his head and went to the corral. His horse had rested enough not to protest more than usual when he saddled her and climbed up. He urged the chestnut horse out and past the door leading down into the sod house. Claire didn't come out. She stood at the base of the steps and watched him ride past.

Slocum put his heels to his horse's flanks. Getting back to the herd seemed more important to him than ever. He didn't cotton to leaving the woman alone, but her problems weren't his. They had shared a night together when both needed it. Slocum kept telling himself that this didn't obligate him toward her none.

He knew he was lying. Even worse, he was lying to himself.

Slocum's eyes turned toward the hazy horizon. He wanted to settle with McKenzie and maybe pay a return call on Claire. He hadn't ridden fifteen minutes when he saw a cloud of dust rising toward Abilene. Reining in, he waited to see what direction the riders went. If they rode from town toward McKenzie's herd, that spelled trouble. From the size of the dust cloud, there might be as many as a dozen men.

Slocum heaved a sigh of relief when he saw that they weren't going in the direction of the drover's camp. He swung around in the saddle and shaded his eyes against the rising sun to get a better view of the riders.

He counted four, but they were riding like twice that number. "They surely are in a hurry to get wherever they're going," he said aloud. He patted his horse on the neck to soothe her. "Wonder where that might be?"

Slocum watched for a few minutes. A rising uneasiness filled him. He didn't know where the Cameron farm was, but Reverend Baskin had ridden off more to the northeast when he'd left the night before. For the world, it looked as if the riders were going directly to Claire Carson's farm.

Indecision struck him. He ought to return to the herd and his work. He had no call sticking his nose in the woman's business. These might be well-wishers from Abilene wanting to help her out. The reverend might have already sent news about Carson's death to town.

It stuck in his craw when he remembered the reception the drovers had gotten from the townsfolk. And Claire had said that no one even bothered to stop by and pay their respects. Why should these four riders drop by now? News of Benjamin Carson's death might have traveled fast—but what response had it caused?

Slocum knew the drunken men he'd talked to on the road were the ones spreading the word. Who else, besides the preacher man, knew of Carson's death?

Slocum wheeled his horse around and started back in no particular hurry to Claire's farm. His suspicions might be wrong. If so, he wouldn't even bother her again. Let the woman work out her grief on her own.

The longer he rode, the more obvious it became that the four riders hadn't kept going. They had stopped in front of the Carson sod house. One remained with the horses. The other three were nowhere to be seen. That meant to Slocum that they had gone inside—with Claire.

He walked his horse into the yard and swept his hat off in a flashy gesture designed to draw attention to himself. He beat some of the dust out of his Stetson and replaced it before speaking. He wanted to give the lone man with the horses plenty of time to realize there wasn't any trouble brewing.

"Morning," Slocum called out. "What's happening here?"

Even with his caution, the man jumped. His hand went towrd his six-shooter, but he stopped short of drawing.

"Who the hell are you?" the man demanded. His thick mustache twitched at the waxed tips, and his long, unkempt beard rippled like wind passing through a wheat field.

"You folks sure aren't the friendliest in the world, are you?" replied Slocum. He turned slightly in the saddle so that his duster moved away from his cross-draw holster. If necessary he could get to the Colt long before this owlhoot drew.

"You're one of them drovers what came into town yesterday—or tried to. You got the diseased beeves."

"Frank McKenzie's herd is as clean as they come," objected Slocum. He wanted to see into the sod house. He heard muffled voices, but the dirt smothered the sounds too well. He knew an argument was raging but couldn't tell what it was about—or if Claire needed his help.

"Ride on out of here, mister. This ain't none of your concern."

"Just wanting to water my horse and see if I can't rustle up a decent meal. The sodbusters around here are more hospitable than you folks from Abilene."

"Get on out of here." The man's words had turned colder than a blue norther blowing out of Canada. He widened his stance and looked as if he'd draw if Slocum ventured another foot closer.

Slocum kept coming. "Don't go making a mistake we'll both be sorry for. Ammunition is damned expensive. I'd hate to waste it on a son of a bitch like you."

Tendons stood out on the man's forearms, and a vein pulsed wildly in his temple. His stance widened even more, and Slocum knew he was getting ready to draw down on him.

"Gus, what in the bloody hell's going on out here?" A man with flame-red hair thrust his head through the house's door. Eyes of polar cold gray locked with Slocum's equally cold green ones. Slocum knew another killer when he saw him.

The first man—Gus—was nothing. Slocum could have gunned him down and never broken out in a sweat. This man, though, wouldn't be that easy.

"Honest, Mr. Trumble, he just rode up. Said he wants water for his horse and a free meal."

"This ain't no charity house, stranger. Turn that nag of yours around and keep on riding."

Slocum dismounted. Cold gray eyes bored into him. He strained to hear movement of gunmetal across leather. Nothing. He turned.

"Your hired hand said it all. I'm looking to water and feed my horse. Something for my own belly would surely be nice. You can't have any objections to me asking the folks who live here."

"How do you know we're not the ones who belong to this spread?" Trumble came up the steps, his left hand staying close to the holster slung on his hip.

"You don't have the look of sodbusters about you. Besides," said Slocum, "I saw your dust cloud settling just as I rode up. You're visitors here too."

"Some men are too damned smart for their own good."

Claire let out a bellow of pain and rage inside the house. She came boiling out, arms thrashing as she shoved away the two remaining men who tried to stop her.

"John, I'm glad you're back." She stumbled and went to one knee, then rushed to him. Slocum had to shift to one side to keep Trumble and his three henchmen in a clear line of fire. If trouble started, he didn't want Claire blocking him.

"Looks as if you're more than a visitor yourself," said Trumble. His cold eyes darted from Claire to Slocum. His left hand moved closer to the holster hanging low on his hip. The fingers began to twitch, as if he was steeling himself to draw.

"They broke in, John. I tried to make them go away, but they wouldn't! They tried to force themselves on me!"

From the corner of his eye Slocum saw that the woman's blouse had been ripped and her skirt had been twisted half around her waist. The men's intent was all too clear. He began to judge his chances of taking all four and saw that they were slim. The man with the horses had moved to one side, and the two from inside the house now stood together like herd animals, unsure of themselves.

Those three posed no problems if shooting started. But Trumble gave every indication of having been in similar situations before. The man carried himself like a gunman. From the tiny twitch at the corner of his lips, he might even enjoy gunning down men.

"You boys try to force yourself on the woman?" Slocum asked in a low, deadly voice. "That's not too hospitable, even for a place like Abilene."

"She don't belong here," Trumble said. "We were trying to convince her to leave peaceable-like."

"They made crazy claims. They said Benjamin had no right to the land. He does! We're homesteading this land!"

Slocum ignored the three gunmen and concentrated on Trumble. The others wouldn't act without their leader's command. Life or death hung on what happened between them.

"Mrs. Carson's got every right to the land."

"Her husband's dead. We seen his grave over there as we rode in," said Trumble. "We came to talk to him about his bad claim. With him dead, that makes it even clearer. A woman can't own land."

"What's this about the claim being bad?" asked Slocum.

"God's truth," spoke up the man with the horses. "The Osage Indians never deeded this over to the government. That makes it illegal for the government to promise it to anybody."

"Much less a woman," finished Trumble. "You see, mister, we're actin' as land agents for the Osage tribe. Just lookin' out for their rights, you might say."

"All the deeds are on file with the land office clerk in Abilene. Benjamin always tended to legal matters. He wouldn't make a mistake like this! He wouldn't!"

"What about the Camerons on the next farm over?" asked Slocum.

"Their claim ain't worth shit, either," Trumble said, savoring the words. "We're on our way over there to tell them, soon as we leave here."

"What do you want from me?" Claire sank to her knees, face buried in cupped hands. Sobs of anger and frustration wracked her body. "Nothing's going right. Nothing!"

"We just want you to get the hell off our land—off the Indians' land," amended Trumble. "I see you got problems, so I'm going to be lenient about it. You got till sundown to clear out."

"Sundown!" Claire shrieked and tore at her hair. Too much had come down on her in the past day to handle.

"I don't think the lady's going to be leaving that fast," said Slocum. "You got a lot of proving to do before she goes. Fact is, this land's about all her late husband had to pass along to her. She's not giving it up without a fight."

Slocum saw Trumble jerk his head to one side. The two men who had been inside the house went for their six-shooters. Slocum moved faster than a striking rattler. His Colt Navy came out of his holster in a blur of speed. The first shot caught one gunman high in the hip, spinning him around. The second shot took off the other's hat, leaving him staring up at the sky in astonishment. His hand had barely touched the butt of his pistol.

Slocum didn't hesitate. He dropped into a crouch just as Trumble's slug whipped past his left ear. Two quick shots in Trumble's direction produced a loud cry of anger and pain.

"Stop it! Stop shooting!" Trumble threw up his hands, six-gun still in his left hand. A trickle of blood oozed down the right side of his face from a grazing shot.

Slocum debated the wisdom of ending this with a single shot through Trumble's rotten head. He had only one shot left in his pistol; when riding, he always carried the Colt with the hammer on an empty cylinder to keep the pistol from accidentally discharging.

"You intend to get on your horses and ride out peacefully?" Slocum asked. His tone carried the hope that Trumble would decide to carry their dispute a mite further.

"We're riding out," said Trumble. "Get out of here, boys." He moved cautiously, aware of Slocum's speed and accuracy, and holstered his pistol. "But you ain't seen the last of us. We got a right to this land, and we're going to take it—one way or another."

"Come with a lawman and some court orders next time," Slocum said. "Otherwise, you won't find the greeting anywhere near as cordial as the one this time."

Trumble rode over and glared down at Slocum. "You're a dead man, cowboy. I never forget."

"Never forget how close you came to getting the top of your head blown off," Slocum replied.

Trumble sneered, touched the bloody crease on his temple and motioned to his three henchmen. They swung their horses around and rode out, heading toward the Cameron farm.

Slocum let the hammer down on the Colt and slammed it back into his holster. He hadn't meant to get this deeply involved in the widow woman's problems. But he had. Now he saw no way of working free without heartache—and maybe death.

Slocum turned and saw the expression on Claire's face. He heaved a deep sigh. A *lot* of heartache lay ahead.

6

Slocum reloaded as Trumble and his henchmen's dust fell back to the Kansas prairie. This time he loaded all six cylinders. On the trail, when he wore his Colt at all, he needed only one shot or at most two for varmints. The civilized variety lurking around Abilene made it necessary to plan for a protracted gunfight.

"Thank you, John. I really hadn't expected to see you again."

"Wouldn't have, except I saw Trumble hightailing it toward your place. Looked like trouble."

"You were right." She wiped the tears from her blue eyes and hugged herself. "They tried to r-rape me!"

"Doubt if they'll be back anytime soon."

"They won't come back as long as you're here."

"Probably won't be back at all," he said. "Whatever they were after won't be solved by banging heads again."

"What do you mean?"

"As cold and cunning as Trumble is, he wasn't behind this. They wanted the farm and seemed willing to throw you off. Why lay claim to the farm at all?"

"But they said the Osage Indians . . ."

"Unless I miss my guess, the Osage don't know squat about Trumble and his doings here. No, he works for someone else. Did your husband get any offers to buy the land?"

Claire shook her head. "He never mentioned any. Besides, the land's not ours until after seven years of proving it. We can stay and no one else is entitled to it, but it's not ours legally."

Slocum nodded. Someone wanted Claire off the land. That put it back into the homestead land bank and allowed some other sodbuster to come along and try to prove it. The only problems Slocum could see with this were that the Carson farm didn't look all that productive—and Trumble was hardly the homesteading sort.

"Ever hear of mining going on around here?"

"No, none."

Slocum hadn't either. That had been a long shot. Outside of some salt mines up north there never been much mining in Kansas. Whatever Trumble's reason for the visit, it would remain hidden. Slocum couldn't discount the notion that Trumble was just out stirring up trouble and maybe looking for someone to rob—or rape.

"John, please don't leave me. Stay here. You said you knew something about farming. Th-this is a good spread. It'll pay off with some hard work. I'm willing."

"I'm going into town for a spell, Claire. Someone's standing behind Trumble, giving orders and looking to profit. I'd like to find out who and why. You'll be safe enough till I get back."

Those words made the woman's face light up. "I'll be waiting for you, John. Anything special I can fix? Something you like and haven't been getting on the drive?"

Her eagerness to please was almost pathetic. The woman had been through hell the past day. He couldn't expect her to lightly dismiss him. He looked to be the only stability she had in the world. With her husband gone, the land might revert to the government, since women weren't allowed to own real property. If Claire had to give up the farm, Slocum didn't see her losing all that much.

"Don't rightly know when I'll be back," he said.

"But you *will* come back, won't you?"

He nodded, then found himself with an armful of woman. She clung to him, then kissed him firmly before allowing him to mount and ride out. He didn't look back; he didn't have to. He felt her eyes on him until he vanished in the morning humidity haze hanging over the prairie waiting to be burned off by the hot Kansas sun.

Slocum was torn between going directly into Abilene to find out about Trumble and returning to McKenzie's herd. He swung around and headed away from town. His duty lay with Frank McKenzie. The man had given him a job for three months, and pay was still owed him. The notion of sixty dollars riding in his pockets drew Slocum as surely as any magnet pulled iron.

He braced for the quarrel that was sure to break out. He had promised to return after Benjamin Carson's funeral and hadn't. Slocum smiled wryly. A night spent with Claire, even under the circumstances, was worth any tongue-lashing McKenzie might give him.

"Where'n the bloody hell you been, Slocum?" came the drover's loud, angry voice as Slocum rode into camp. "We thought those yahoos from town had drygulched you."

"Look at 'im," said another cowboy. "Looks like a kitten with a saucer of cream."

"Kitten?" asked another. "Looks like a pussy-smile to me. He's been out cattin' around, ain't you, John?"

Slocum ignored the crude comments. He dismounted and went to talk with McKenzie.

"Damned if I don't think they're right. You been out whorin' while we've been working?"

"Nothing of the sort," Slocum said. "I buried the sod-buster, got a preacher man to say words over the grave, and then ran into some trouble. You weren't far wrong when you said some of the townsfolk might try to drygulch me."

"Lemme see your six-shooter." McKenzie held out his hand. Slocum's eyes locked with the drover's. He silently passed over the Colt. McKenzie sniffed at the muzzle, then handed it back. "Been fired, all right. You wing any of the bastards?"

"Creased one about here," said Slocum, pointing to a spot on his hip. "Grazed their leader on the side of the head."

"How many?"

Slocum found himself telling the story to the gathered company of cowboys. When he finished, McKenzie blurted, "We ought to ride into that damned town and burn it to the ground! They can't treat us like that! By damn, we're Texans!"

The enthusiasm for this simple statement made Slocum wary. He took McKenzie by the arm and got the drover where he could talk privately. "What's happened? They surely are stirred up over something."

McKenzie cleared his throat, looked around, and then said, "We got word from the town that they're not going to let us bring the herd any closer. They're so fearful of Spanish fever there's even talk of coming out and destroying my beeves. By God, I'll kill everyone in Abilene if they try a damnfool thing like that."

Slocum scratched his head. Cow towns lived or died on the number of cattle passing through. Merchants starved without drovers to sell supplies to—and cowboys to liquor

"What are you doing out here? Why aren't you tending the herd?" Slocum looked around. There couldn't be more than ten men left with the entire herd. McKenzie had another eight with him.

"We're looking for a spot to graze the herd. Marshal Lewis came out and told us he'd got complaints about our beeves destroying private property. Seems we had camped on someone's land and they weren't about to let us stay one second longer. No damned compassion anywhere in this town, much less justice."

Slocum nodded. He saw how they were being caught in the jaws of a steel trap. The townspeople thought the cattle herd was rife with Spanish fever and wouldn't allow sale. The railroad went along with this, not wanting to spread a nonexistent disease. The only way of selling the beeves was in letting them stay in quarantine, but McKenzie didn't have the money for feed.

Three months of quarantine would insure that his drovers would never be paid, too. The high cost would eat into any slim profits the Texan might make.

Someone would waltz away with the herd and a nice profit, and it wouldn't be the owner or the men who had worked so hard getting the longhorns to market.

"We got to move by sundown or the marshal's going to seize the herd," McKenzie said.

"All you need is grassland?" asked Slocum.

"You know that," snapped McKenzie. The drover cocked his head to one side and looked at Slocum. "If you got a place for us to put the herd, speak up."

"Let me do some talking about this." Slocum jumped down from the low-roofed house and went inside. Claire cowered against the back wall, a knife in her hand.

"What's happening, John?"

"Nothing to get hot and bothered over. In fact, this might be a boon to us all." He sat down on the single chair and got his thoughts in order. Everything fell neatly into place. "How would you like to make a few dollars and not have to do anything for it?"

"How?" Suspicion flared.

"Let Mr. McKenzie graze his herd on your land. Your husband hadn't started tilling yet. The land is mostly grass, which is just fine for the longhorns."

"They'll pay?"

Slocum nodded. "The problem is that payment might be delayed a mite." He explained the dilemma McKenzie found himself in.

"The grass doesn't cost me anything. The land is all I've got." Her blue eyes locked with his green ones. "This means you'll be around more, won't it?"

"Could be," he said lightly. "Mostly, though, I'm going to be in town. We got a long, hard fight ahead of us."

"No gunplay!"

"Not that kind of fight. The marshal seems an honest enough man, but the law dictates he go against our needs. I think Frank and I can do something to change that around."

"Why?"

"I got a name from the Osage Indians. In town I might be able to track down the owner of that name and find out if he's the one behind all our troubles."

Claire looked as if she were in real pain. "I don't want you going away for long, John. You're the best thing that's happened to me since I came to Kansas."

"I'll see what Frank has to say. The drovers won't bother you none. They'll keep the longhorns away from the land that's already been tilled. Might even get them to help out with the chores, since it's going to be a spell before you see any money."

She shrugged, her expression bleak.

Slocum hurried outside. The heat hit him like a hammer blow. Another hour would see it unbearable in the direct sun. McKenzie and the others had dismounted and were lounging about on the shady side of the house.

"Well?"

"It's worked out, Mr. McKenzie. You can use this land if you agree to pay what's fair after you collect."

"Hard to say what's fair, since we don't know how long they're going to hold the herd hostage." McKenzie slapped his knee and declared, "Done. I can't afford to quibble. I might not make a thin dime off this drive, but by damn I'm not going to lose any money, either. I'm going to sell my beeves and get them to market, and the devil can take the hindmost!"

"Let's move the herd. I told the lady they wouldn't get into the plowed fields. Not much for them to eat there, anyway. The crops didn't get planted right and haven't sprouted."

"We can avoid the fields. There's a patch of grassy plains just over there that might do us for a week or more. By then we can either move on or have this settled." McKenzie's hand brushed across the six-shooter slung at his side. Slocum knew what the drover planned. If legal means didn't work, they would resort to force.

Slocum wasn't about to tell McKenzie that it wouldn't work. He understood the frustration the man felt. It was building to the boiling point inside him, too. For no good reason, someone had bushwhacked him, and for that someone would pay in blood.

"It'll take about an hour getting the beeves over here," said McKenzie. "After that, I want to head back into town and argue a bit more."

Dykstra and that Doc Pendleton had a lock on the beef trade in Abilene, or so it seemed. Someone else had to be involved, though. Neither man had the guts or brains to work the swindle they were working on McKenzie.

Slocum saddled up and rode off with the others, aware that Claire was watching him until they were all out of sight. The other cowboys muttered among themselves, occasionally glancing in his direction. He knew what they were saying. And he wasn't sure if they weren't right. He was one lucky son of a bitch spending time with the pretty widow woman, but it might not be the smartest thing in the world to do. He might find himself tangled up when he ought to be riding on. Slocum still didn't know if this was a good thing.

McKenzie rode close to Slocum. "I'm at a loss what to do about this, short of shooting up the town."

"Marshal Lewis wouldn't take kindly to that. There's one man behind all our trouble. We find out who he is and everything will fall into place for us."

"You willing to kill to get your wages?"

Slocum looked at McKenzie. "It hasn't come to that yet. If it does, I reckon I am." Slocum didn't mention that he had killed for a lot less provocation. Memories of the bloody, brutal days with Quantrill's Raiders flashed through his head. They had killed for the pleasure of it— and it had sickened him.

"Found out a bit more about the situation." Slocum told McKenzie about the Osage selling parcels of land.

"This is the prime grassland," McKenzie said. "Fatten beeves up on it and ship 'em off to Chicago and you can make a fortune."

"Even more of a fortune if you don't have competition," said Slocum. "Looks as if someone's trying to get it all. Fatten the cattle, ship them—and own the land around Abilene."

"There's more railroads coming in. Heard tell that the Kansas Pacific was getting some competition from the AT&SF. Might be more'n that intendin' to put in track."

This tickled Slocum's memory. He almost had the answer to the problem gnawing away in his gut. But the elusive answer faded, like the cool wind promised by the prairie and never delivered.

By now they had arrived back at the herd. "All right, boys. Get these beeves moving. We got company to watch to be sure we do it right." McKenzie put spurs to his horse and trotted off. Slocum followed. They reined in by Marshal Lewis and his deputy, Lem Washington.

"See you're taking my warning to heart. I like that," Lewis said, working at the chaw in his jowl. He spat before saying, "Reckon the only question is, where you drivin' the cows? Can't let you go spreading the Texas fever around the countryside. They'd have my ears nailed to the barn door for sure if'n I did a thing like that."

"We got permission from a homesteader," said McKenzie. "You can ask her. We got grazing rights till we get these beeves sold."

"Her? You meanin' the widow Carson? Reverend Baskin told me she was pinin' away something fierce."

Slocum stiffened at the implication that Claire wanted nothing more than to screw two dozen horny drovers. McKenzie motioned him to silence. Lewis's eyes darted from one man to the other.

"Ain't said something I shouldn't have, have I? Always getting people riled over nothing. Apologize, if I have."

"No offense taken, Marshal."

"There's something of a problem with grazing these longhorns on the widow's land. It ain't hers. Not legally. Women can't own property, and her being a widow and all . . ."

"Who's objecting to it? Trumble?"

"Haven't heard from him."

"But you have heard from his boss, haven't you?" demanded Slocum.

"You must be a mind reader. Saw one of them once. Came through with a snake oil salesman and a hootchy-kootchy dancer. Got no idea how he done it, but I swear to God, he was able to know what was in my mind. Just like he had the newspaper open and was lookin' at the headlines, it was. Ran the bastard out of town on general principles."

"Does Hammerschmidt have claim to the land?" Slocum asked.

"Reckon he might. He's been real active buyin' up land all around town lately." Lewis squinted as he stared at Slocum. "Now how did you come to know that Trumble works for Mr. Hammerschmidt?"

"Isn't he part of the railroad?"

"He's a director of the Kansas Pacific," said Lewis. "Don't go getting Josiah Hammerschmidt's dander up. He's never been known as a peaceable man when crossed. Goes to show you can't believe all them stories about fat men being jolly. Nastiest man I ever saw when crossed."

Slocum pulled his horse around and rode off without another word. He knew who was behind their trouble now. And it all seemed logical. Hammerschmidt intended to get a stranglehold on Abilene by using the railroad as a lever.

Cattle, land, railroad—the director of the Kansas Pacific would own it all unless stopped.

Slocum didn't know if he would be able to do that, but he knew he could make it uncomfortable enough for Hammerschmidt to at least collect his wages and get McKenzie's longhorns sold.

10

"They don't look any too friendly," said Kelly, riding beside Slocum.

"No reason for them to. They figure the longhorns are carrying the fever." Slocum eyed the homesteader with the shotgun and felt the man's hot gaze in return. On impulse, Slocum rode over. He tipped his hat in the man's direction.

"What you want?" the sodbuster called out. His fingers worked over the trigger guard. If he didn't go to playing with the triggers on the double-barreled shotgun, Slocum knew he was safe.

"We're driving our herd through to Miz Carson's farm. She's letting us use her unplowed land as a feed lot."

"Don't go getting them sick longhorns on my property. You keep 'em out there on the road."

"No disease among these. That's a rumor." Slocum smiled crookedly. He added, "That's a mean rumor Mr.

Hammerschmidt started. He wants to buy up the beeves cheap so he can make a bigger profit."

From the way the farmer jumped, Slocum knew he had touched a raw nerve. "You have dealings with Josiah Hammerschmidt?" he asked.

"Not if I can damned well help it," snapped the sodbuster. "That son of a bitch tried to run me off my land. He sent around them gunslingers of his. I run 'em off. Told 'em I'd blow their fool heads off if I saw them poking up over the horizon, I did!"

"Good for you. Seems to me that Hammerschmidt is biting off more than he can chew."

"You know about that?"

"He's got some land from the Indians that about boxes you in, unless I miss my guess."

"Told ole Buffalo Pizzle not to deal with him, but the damned redskin wouldn't listen. The damned railroad's going to own all our souls before Hammerschmidt's finished with us."

"Jesse, you stop swearin'. You promised the reverend you wouldn't talk like that no more."

"Sorry, Sarah." The farmer looked sheepish and lowered his shotgun. "The woman's got it stuck in her craw about cussin'."

"Hammerschmidt's enough to make a saint say a few choice words," Slocum said.

"Reckon you might be right on that subject." The sodbuster looked at the cattle passing by along the rutted road. "They don't look to be carrying the fever."

"The only ones we had to destroy broke their fool legs in prairie dog holes. All are healthy."

"You men want something to drink? Don't have much. Sarah's fixed up some lemonade."

Even though the farmer spoke in a normal voice, the words carried from one side of the herd to the other. Men flocked over.

"Won't take anything that fine," said Slocum, giving the cowboys a hard look. "But we'd be much obliged if we could get some water."

"No problem. And if you want to use the stock pond for your longhorns, it's about a mile in that direction." The farmer pointed.

"Wouldn't want to use your precious water," spoke up Frank McKenzie.

"No need to fret none on that score," the man said. "Look at the sky. See how the clouds are building up? We're in for one hell of a storm if those goddamned anvil-topped ones are any sign."

"Jesse!"

"Sorry, Sarah."

Slocum had noticed the black clouds and wondered if they carried any rain. The farmer lived or died by knowing such things. They must be in store for a real frog strangler if he was allowing an entire herd of thirsty longhorns to use his stock pond.

Slocum tipped his hat in the woman's direction, then dismounted and brushed off some of the trail dust. "Don't care what your husband calls it, any storm is going to be a blessing."

"Don't count on it, mister."

"Slocum," he supplied. The woman smiled and handed him a battered tin cup. He noticed it had lemonade in it. He wasn't about to refuse, even if McKenzie had rightly told his men not to take any such lagniappe from the home-steaders. The lemonade went down his throat and settled coolly in his belly. It tasted better than any whiskey.

"Mr. Slocum, what do you know about Josiah Hammerschmidt's plans?" The woman looked concerned, a frown wrinkling her forehead. Slocum reckoned she had a right to be upset over the railroad director's actions.

"He seems to be taking advantage of Joe McCoy being out of town."

"Back east," supplied the farmer.

"Heard New York City from his agent." Slocum finished the lemonade and refused a refill, preferring to drink the water. He wouldn't take advantage of these people's generosity.

"Dykstra." The farmer spat. "That son of a bitch."

Slocum noticed that his wife didn't reproach him this time for his language. From the way her lips moved silently, she might have been mouthing the same curse.

"Didn't figure he was too well liked in these parts."

"He's never done anything outright to annoy us, but I heard rumors. Him and that worthless drunk Doc Pendleton are in cahoots with Hammerschmidt. But I figure you know all about that."

"Doesn't take long to hear the stories," Slocum allowed. "You folks ought to get to speaking with your neighbors. A protective association might be what you need to hold off the likes of Hammerschmidt."

"Wouldn't do any good. He's got the law in his hip pocket."

"Seems as if your marshal's an honest enough man. Law seems more important to him than offending a rich man, even a powerful director of the railroad."

"The Kansas Pacific is the heart of this land grab," avowed the woman. "They want to steal all this land and turn it into fattening pens. That would save them grain cost and the need to drive the cattle another dozen miles into Abilene."

"You homesteaders kept out the longhorns *with* Spanish fever," said Slocum. "You might be able to do something about a different kind of disease."

"Cows ain't got the money Josiah Hammerschmidt's got."

"And longhorns don't have the kind of bosses he must. He doesn't own the railroad, does he?"

"Owns a portion. Not all, from what I hear. He's been

trying to put in his own spur in these parts for some time."

Slocum began to understand. Hammerschmidt was playing every side against the other. He was accumulating land in any way possible to build the fattening pens—and those pens would supply his own rail line cattle to be sold to the larger Kansas Pacific. Hammerschmidt looked to make a profit on every transaction along the way.

"Much obliged for the hospitality," he said.

"You look like a man searching for trouble," the woman said.

"No, ma'am. I think it's the other way around. Trouble's found me and I just want to put things right." Slocum mounted. He looked down at Jesse and Sarah. "You folks might want to look in on the widow Carson. She's having a hard time of it. She's a proud lady, so don't go offering charity, but a helping hand would be appreciated, I'm sure."

Slocum wheeled his horse around and rejoined the cowboys as they herded the longhorns toward Claire's farm. It took the better part of the afternoon to get them watered at the stock pond and put to grazing on the dry grass. By then the thunderheads had built up directly overhead and Slocum began to worry about tornadoes.

"Looking like it'll get wet soon," said McKenzie. "And for one, I'm damned glad of it. I'm sick of eating dust all day long."

"You be needing me?" Slocum asked.

McKenzie eyed him, then shook his head. "You keep out of trouble. I don't want to try to sweet-talk the marshal into letting you out of jail."

"I'm not looking for that to happen, Mr. McKenzie."

"They never do." McKenzie laughed. "Hell and damnation, I know you won't go gettin' liquored up and shoot the town to splinters. You spent your last dollar buyin' me that beer at the Alamo."

Slocum grinned. "Reckon that's so. I'll be back before morning."

"That's just about when you're due to go back on patrol. You may not be getting paid, but that don't mean you can weasel out of workin' this herd."

Slocum took the drover's words as a joke. From the way McKenzie looked, Slocum wasn't too sure if that was the right thing to do. McKenzie alternated between crazy optimism on selling his beeves soon and kettle-black despair over being unable to pay his hands.

He hadn't ridden a mile toward Abilene when the first heavy drops of rain hit. They stung with the power of their fall from the towering thunderhead. Slocum reined in and fumbled in his roll to pull out his yellow slicker. He barely had it on when the rain came in earnest. In seconds, the dry, dusty road turned to ankle-deep mud. His horse gamely sloughed through it, but both horse and rider were pleased to reach town.

Slocum found an overhang and rode under it. Dismounting, he stood and stared at the sheets of rain coming down. He wouldn't have believed they'd been in the middle of a drought if the past hour was all he'd seen of Kansas. He left his horse under the shelter and went to poke around. He had no real notion where to start or what he wanted to do.

Josiah Hammerschmidt had a hand in McKenzie's and the homesteaders' troubles. The railroad director had to have left behind a trail that would lead to proof of his underhanded scheming.

Slocum trudged along toward the land office, intending to see if Hammerschmidt had bought up any other land. From this he hoped to piece together the proposed route of the man's new railroad spur. He didn't get halfway down Main street when he heard a commotion in front of Grove's General Store.

He paused to watch and saw a sandy-haired sodbuster knocked flat on his ass. The farmer stood, only to be knoced down again. This time he stumbled backward and landed in the muddy street.

Three men came out of the store and stood just under the porch roof, laughing at the farmer's plight.

"Don't that beat all, Gus?" came a voice Slocum remembered all too well. He didn't have to see the mussed-up bright red hair or the cruel smile to know Trumble.

"Can't even walk without fallin' over his own damned boots!" crowed Gus. "Get your ass out of the street, Cameron. You're provin' an obstacle for the horses. Hate to have them damage their hooves kickin' at your clumsy carcass!"

Trumble and his two henchmen laughed uproariously at this. Cameron fought to get to his feet but slipped in the slick mud. He made a huge splash, then wiggled around, getting muddier and madder. Slocum saw the man struggling to pull a pistol he had tucked into the waistband of his canvas drawers.

The set of Trumble's body told the story. If the sodbuster got his hog-let out, he would be gunned down on the spot.

"Trumble!" Slocum shouted again, to be sure he was heard over the cascading rain. He strode along the rickety boardwalk and stopped, a muddy patch between him and the gunman.

Trumble glanced from Cameron back to Slocum. He saw where the real danger lay. He half turned and faced Slocum.

"You thinkin' you're lucky today, widow-fucker?"

Slocum didn't rise to the gross insult. To lose his temper now would give Trumble an edge. He had never seen the gunman in action, but he guessed he must be good. He doubted a man as rich as Josiah Hammerschmidt would hire second-rate talent.

Slocum's attention rested on Trumble, but he saw the

other two out of the corner of his eye. Gus's expression
was one of sheer fright.

"You didn't do a very good job bushwhacking me,"
Slocum said. He slowly reached into his vest pocket and
found the spent shell casing. He flipped it toward Trumble.
The brass rattled to a halt at the man's feet.

Trumble snapped something that was drowned out by a
clap of thunder. Gus's reply came through loud and clear,
confirming what Slocum had already guessed.

". . . don't know how he done it, boss. Honest! I made a
clean shot!"

"You couldn't hit the broad side of a barn if you were
locked inside, Gus," Slocum said.

"You mealymouthed cowpuncher!" Gus went for his
gun. Slocum's hand twitched, but he didn't draw. He saw
Cameron getting his pistol free at last. The farmer fired,
the shot digging a hole in the wood post beside Trumble's
head.

The gunman didn't flinch or move. His pale gray eyes
fixed on the real threat: John Slocum.

"Take care of that sodbuster, Gus, Pete. I got work of
my own to do."

When Gus went for his six-shooter, Slocum acted. He
couldn't let them murder the homesteader. Hand flashing
for his Colt Navy, he drew and got off a quick, accurate
shot that brought a cry of pain and rage to Gus's lips.

"The bastard shot me!" cried Gus. He clutched at his
wounded right arm. The one called Pete dragged out a
sawed-off shotgun he had dangling from a rope around his
shoulder.

Slocum's second and third shots made sure that the
deadly scattergun never found a decent target. Pete sank to
his knees, eyes open in shock and his face slack. He was
dead before he toppled face-down into the muddy street.

"I'll get you, Trumble. You can't do this to me!" The
sodbuster screamed threats as he struggled to cock his pis-

tol again. "You've made a fool out of me for the last time!"

Cameron's next shot vanished into the wall of falling water. Trumble paid it no mind. He was going for his own pistol—and Slocum was getting behind a water barrel to keep from stopping a slug in the belly.

Trumble's marksmanship was everything Slocum thought it would be. Three slugs accurately dug their way through the top of the water barrel, barely missing Slocum's head. He was glad that Trumble had sent Gus out to bushwhack him. If the gunman had done the job himself, Slocum knew his bones would have been picked clean by prairie hawks by now.

"You can't come into town and kill innocent men," Trumble shouted, trying to draw him out. "We hang murderers in Abilene."

Slocum chanced a quick look around the side of the barrel. Trumble had moved to the edge of the general store. He had positioned himself well. No matter how he tried, Slocum would never be able to get a clean shot at the gunman.

"Cameron!" Slocum bellowed. "Get the hell out of the way!"

His brief glance had shown him that the farmer still stood in the center of the street, working frantically to cock his ungainly ancient pistol again. From the trouble the man had with it, Slocum was worried that it might blow up in his face.

"Take care of him, Gus." Trumble's voice was cold, deadly—and pitched to draw out Slocum.

Gus moved to a spot just under the porch and raised his pistol, using his left hand to support his wounded right. Only this prevented him from getting a killing shot in on Cameron.

Slocum cursed, cocked his Colt, and dove into the street, rolling through the filth and praying that the water and mud didn't clog the Colt's precision mechanism. He fired twice more, both shots finding Gus's belly. The man's shot went wild. He sat down heavily on the wood walkway, clutching his guts and howling in pain.

"Goodbye," said Trumble, moving out into the rain. The water ran in rivers from the broad brim of his hat. He lifted his pistol and pointed it at Slocum. The muzzle looked big enough to crawl into.

Slocum lifted his pistol and fired the last round. The recoil felt good; he knew the bullet would find its target.

The startled look on Trumble's face told the story. The gunman had assumed that Slocum carried his pistol with the hammer safely resting on an empty chamber, just as he and most other men who wore six-shooters all the time did.

Even as the surprise showed on Trumble's face, Slocum knew he hadn't got in a killing shot. He dived back into the mud and rolled, a slug narrowly missing his skull.

"Die, you son of a bitch! Die!" Cameron had gone berserk. He stood in the middle of the street in the pouring rain, trying to fire again at Trumble. He seemed oblivious to the danger he was in. Slocum hit him low, just below the knees. The sodbuster folded up like a buck knife and splashed into the street, struggling and shrieking.

Slocum found the man's fallen pistol and rolled, trying to give Trumble as small a target as possible.

He came to a sitting position, Cameron's old pistol resting uncomfortably in his hand. He didn't know if the long hexagonal barrel had clogged with mud and would explode. He didn't even know if there were any rounds left in the gun.

Slocum slumped. He didn't have to find out if the gun would explode and blow his hand off. Trumble had vanished into the falling rain, leaving behind his two henchmen.

11

Slocum felt like a damned fool sitting in the rain with the sodbuster's heavy pistol in his hand. He wiped the rain from his eyes and tried to see where Trumble had gone. The man had vanished down the alley, leaving Gus and Pete behind. Pete lay in the mud, face-down and not moving. Slocum had finished him off. Gus tried to crawl away, still clutching at his abdomen. He twitched and jerked and didn't make much progress in the slippery mud of the street.

By this time men were poking their heads out curiously to see who had died. A man emerged from the general store and took in the situation. Slocum saw the slow smile cross his face. At least one citizen in Abilene was happy with this gunfight's result.

"You still in one piece?" Slocum called out to Cameron.

The farmer sat a few feet away, unmoving, his eyes fixed on Pete's body. "I killed him. I shot him."

"You didn't even come close," Slocum said with ill-disguised contempt. If a man pulled a six-shooter on another, he ought to be able to use it. Cameron had made a botch of this and might have ended up dead. If Slocum hadn't come by, Trumble would have blown his fool head off.

"I shot him."

Slocum got to his feet and wiped off some of the mud. It was a losing proposition. He let the rain carry off the muddy rivers and return the dirt to the street where it belonged. He helped Cameron up. The sodbuster moved as if he had gone into shock. Slocum guided him to the porch in front of the general store. There wasn't any need for them to tolerate the rain beating down on their heads.

"You surely are a caution with that pistol," spoke up the man standing in the general store's doorway. "If I hadn't seen all that had happened, I'd've thought they had a falling out and shot up one another."

Slocum digested this information. The townspeople obviously thought the worst of Trumble and his cohorts. Being good with a gun had put him—temporarily—in cahoots with Trumble.

"Did you get hit?" Slocum asked of Cameron. The sandy-haired farmer shook his head, sending droplets flying in all directions.

"Don't reckon I did. I . . . I just blew up. They have no right to push me around like that. They been doing it to everybody in this damned town for too long."

"He'll be fine," the store owner assured Slocum. "How about yourself? You look to be bleeding from a head wound."

Slocum touched the spot where Gus had winged him days earlier. Claire's fresh bandage had come loose in the fracas, and the rain had washed away the scab.

"An old injury. Doesn't amount to much."

"I heard what they said. Did they try to bushwhack you?"

Slocum involuntarily touched the shallow, bloody groove on the side of his head. This was answer enough for the few men who had gathered around to see what was going on.

"What do you think we should do with that one?" The man speaking pointed to Gus, who had reached the edge of the porch and had flopped back over the edge into a mud puddle. Pain showed in every line of the man's weather-beaten face. Slocum knew a gut wound might fester and take weeks to kill him. He felt no sympathy. Gus had tried to back-shoot him and had got what he deserved.

"Suppose we ought to get Doc Pendleton. He wouldn't mind looking after one of his own kind." The store owner spat in Gus's direction. He missed. The expression on his face showed he was considering a second gobbet, then decided against it. "One of you go find Doc."

"Better get Marshal Lewis, too," said Slocum. "He's got to clean up the street." He indicated Pete.

"Lewis only takes care of dead critters—horses, mules, animals that have keeled over and got left by their owners."

"That description fits *that*." Slocum didn't try to hide his disgust. He sat down in a straight-backed wood chair and began knocking the mud from the barrel of Cameron's pistol. He was glad he hadn't tried firing it. The clogged barrel would have taken off his hand and maybe his head.

He threw down the pistol and pulled his own precision weapon from the soft leather cross-draw holster. The Colt hadn't gotten too mucked up in the fight. He worked quickly and efficiently to scour out the barrel and to re-charge the cylinders. A small cluster of men gathered around in a semicircle to watch.

"What is it?" he asked, looking up.

"You goin' after Trumble?"

The coldness in his eyes spoke more eloquently than any words. Slocum shoved the Colt Navy into his holster and stood. The crowd parted for him. Looking around the corner showed nothing he hadn't expected: rain barrels filled with runoff from the building roofs and mud deepening in the alley. Of Trumble he saw no trace.

"Where's that owlhoot likely to go?"

"He roosts over at the Alamo Saloon," spoke up someone toward the back of the crowd. "You might want to hold on a second, mister. The marshal's making his way across the street."

Slocum didn't want to answer lengthy questions. Let Cameron deal with those. In his dazed condition, the man might even take credit for all the mayhem. Slocum knew that wouldn't last long, if it happened. Too many others had witnessed the shoot-out and knew who was responsible.

He hurried down the alley, ready to go for the ebony-handled six-shooter the instant he saw Trumble. The outlaw was nowhere to be seen.

Slocum came out into another Abilene street that looked exactly like the one he had left. He stepped up onto the boardwalk and slowly made his way toward the Alamo Saloon. Every sense came alive. He heard sounds too small to otherwise detect. His keen eyes looked behind barrels and in doorways, hunting for the elusive Trumble. Slocum even thought he could taste the trouble brewing—and it left a bitter tang on his tongue.

The broad etched-glass doors in front of the Alamo Saloon stood wide open. Slocum saw movement inside but couldn't identify the men. He walked to the side of the building and peered down the side street. The rain had driven everyone indoors. Satisfied that it would take several seconds for anyone to circle behind him and come from the rear of the saloon, he went in.

He stood with his back to the door as he studied those

milling about in the large room. Two men he had never seen before were bellied up to the bar. One had been there for some time, if the degree of his drunkenness was any measure. The other frowned but said nothing, turning back to his shot of whiskey.

Doc Pendleton and the cattle agent Dykstra sat at a green-felt-covered poker table in the center of the room, a half-empty bottle of rye whiskey between them. Both had been drinking heavily. Neither looked concerned at Slocum's presence.

Slocum walked over to their table. "Where's Trumble?"

"Why should we know?" asked Dykstra. For all the liquor he had apparently consumed—and spilled down the crimson silk cravat he wore—his voice wasn't slurred. Slocum noted, though, that his hand shook.

"I just gunned down Pete," Slocum said. Neither showed any surprise at this. Slocum knew that Trumble had been here. Some small outrage would have been in order if they'd wanted to carry through with their charade of innocence. "And Gus has a couple slugs in his fat gut."

"Doc, I told you that drovers bring the worst in a town. Murder, shooting, where will it all end?"

"Get rid of the cowboys and that might help maintain the peace around town," the doctor said. His eyes were bloodshot. Slocum guessed that he might be the one consuming the bulk of the rotgut whiskey. "This young buck is looking for a fight."

"Trumble. I want him. Where is he?"

"Have a drink, mister. You look like you need something to steady your nerves," said Dykstra. His hand now shook uncontrollably as he tried to pour the drink. He spilled much of it onto the table.

Slocum heard sounds behind him. He whirled around, went into a crouch, and whipped out his Colt, ready to fire. Only his swift reflexes saved Marshal Lewis from getting a slug between the eyes.

"What's going on in here?" the marshal boomed. He paid no attention to Slocum's tense stance. When the lawman walked forward, Slocum relaxed and put his six-gun back into its holster.

"This yahoo came in lookin' for a fight, Marshal. Do something about him, will you? Honest citizens can't even get a peaceable drink anymore." Doc Pendleton knocked back a full shot of whiskey and poured another. Slocum noted that his hands were steady. Only Dykstra showed the strain.

"What's your problem, son? Can't you act like anything but a wild man after bein' on the trail for so long?"

"You know what happened over at Grove's Store."

"Came from there."

"I want Trumble. He tried to gun down Cameron. He damned near shot me, too."

"Don't see that you're any the worse for wear and tear. As to Mr. Cameron, he's on his way back to his farm. Can't say he's able to say much that means anything, but the eyewitnesses claim you and them other two had at it good and proper."

"Trumble—" began Slocum.

"Trumble was never mentioned."

Slocum looked past the marshal and caught a reflection in the long mirror over the bar. He swung around, hand flashing with lightning speed to his Colt. He drew and fired in one smooth motion. The man at the head of the stairs ducked back. The slug tore away at the doorjamb, sending splinters flying.

Slocum took a step, only to find Marshal Lewis's strong hand on his wrist, wrestling the Colt up. The lawman's other arm circled Slocum's throat and bent him backward. A hard knee drove into the middle of his spine, insuring his cooperation.

"Can't let you go around shooting up saloons, either. Bad for business."

"Trumble's upstairs!"

"Might be. I got no real quarrel with him—and you don't, either, 'cuz I say you don't. Come along peaceable-like, son, or I'll break your damnfool neck."

Slocum had no choice but to let the marshal manhandle him. He was swung about and shoved toward the door. He caught sight of Trumble for a final time in the mirror. The man stood at the head of the stairs sneering at him. In front of the Alamo, Lewis wrested the Colt from his hand.

"I'll keep this for the time being." He tucked it securely into his belt. "Let's go on over to the jail and have a little talk about disturbin' the peace."

Slocum started to argue, then saw the black deputy standing silently beside the saloon door, a shotgun resting in the crook of his left arm. All it would take would be a single upward movement of a few inches to bring the deadly weapon to bear. Slocum didn't hanker to have his guts blown out into the muddy street. He jerked free of the marshal's grip and walked toward the jail, fuming.

Inside, he sat in a chair while Lewis and the deputy stood on either side. Lewis said, "You can't go around shooting down everyone you don't like, son. On the trail it might be different. We're tryin' to bring some civilization to Abilene."

"Trumble would have killed Cameron."

"Might have, if he'd been there. Trumble's one nasty hombre. You'll never hear me say otherwise. Eyewitnesses said you and Gus and Pete and Mr. Cameron were involved over at the store. Can't rightly decide what happened since no two of 'em told the same story. Unless someone says different, we'll just forget that."

"Good." Slocum got to his feet. Lewis shoved him back down.

"Not so fast, son. We got another charge against you. Disturbin' the peace. You tried to shoot up the Alamo Saloon in my presence. I might not be able to figure out what happened in front of Grove's Store but I *saw* you destroyin' private property." Lewis laid Slocum's pistol on his desk. "Got to lock you up."

"Marshall—"

"Lem, show our guest into the Presidential Suite. And if he gives you any lip, use the shotgun on him."

Slocum went silently into the rear of the jail without further protest. He saw it wouldn't get him anywhere. He sat in the simple steel-barred cage and stewed for over two hours before he heard voices in the marshal's outer office.

"Don't know if I ought to be doin' this," Lewis said, coming through the door into the cell area. "Look at 'im. A dyed-in-the-wool criminal, if I ever saw one."

Slocum did not appreciate the lawman's joking tone. To Lewis this was nothing. To Slocum, it meant Trumble could be on the train and heading for parts unknown.

"Can't argue the point none, Marshal," said Frank McKenzie. "But he is one of my cowboys. Feel responsible for him, even if I'm not legally bound to bail him out."

"From what I hear, you couldn't buy warm spit with twice the money you got in your wallet," observed the marshal. "That's why I think I'm doing you a big favor lettin' him go without postin' any bond."

"I'll keep him out of Abilene," promised McKenzie.

Slocum almost spoke his mind. No one dictated to him. If he wanted Trumble—and he did—no one would stop him. But he saw that he might rot in the cell if Lewis didn't get some promise of peace around town.

"We're not that bad off," said McKenzie. "We got grazing rights for as long as it takes to convince you we're not carrying Spanish fever."

"There's too much going on around town that I don't understand," admitted Lewis. "That don't stop me from wonderin', though." He stared at Slocum. "Don't look too repentant, does he?"

"He won't get into any more trouble," promised McKenzie.

"That right, son?"

"I won't start anything," Slocum said. He left it unspoken that he would finish what Trumble had already started.

Lewis snorted. "Don't amount to much of a promise, does it? Still, I don't want to bother with feedin' a prisoner. Our funds aren't fallin' out of the strongbox and onto the floor, after all. Hell, if I didn't serve process at five dollars a day, I wouldn't make but fifty a month—and they pay in those worthless greenbacks."

On this point Slocum and the marshal rode common ground. Neither trusted scrip.

Marshal Lewis unlocked the cell door and swung it open. "You get on out of town. I don't want to see you around here again—ever."

"Might need his help when I sell the beeves," said McKenzie.

"Use him however you like. Just don't let me catch him in Abilene. If I do, it's a three-dollar fine for disturbin' the peace—and another ten for pissin' me off."

The marshal stalked back into his office. When Slocum reached for his six-shooter, Lewis snatched it away. "Don't go gettin' greedy, son. I don't want you carryin' this in town." He thrust it butt first toward Frank McKenzie. The drover took it, looked at Slocum as if to say "This isn't my doing," and then stuffed it into his belt.

"You can get it from him when you're out of my sight and not one second before," said Lewis. "You been told my likes and dislikes. Get out of here, and make sure you don't cross me again."

"Thanks, Marshal. This is a real nice thing you're doing for Slocum." McKenzie grabbed Slocum's arm and steered him toward the door. In a low voice, he said, "Let's get the hell out of here before he throws us both in a cell."

Slocum stood just outside the marshal's office in the rain. The sky continued to open up and vent forth its liquid wrath. A lightning bolt arched across the sky and sent a peal of thunder rolling down the street.

"He's a good man. He could have let you rot in there. Among the whole crew, I couldn't have raised three dollars. You're damned lucky I came into town to try to talk with Dykstra again."

"Thanks, Mr. McKenzie. But I'm not going to let Trumble get away with this."

"Let's get our horses. We can talk about it while we ride."

McKenzie took a step into the street just as a vivid green lightning bolt lit up the sky above. For a second, Slocum thought it was only thunder he heard. Then he realized that a sharper report had sounded almost simultaneously with the roar.

Frank McKenzie straightened. His prominent cheekbones cast shadows on his face as his lips tried to form words. He sank to his knees, then fell face-down in the mud.

A second bullet crashed into the splintery post just behind Slocum. He reached for his pistol, then remembered McKenzie still had it tucked away in his belt.

The third shot tore away part of his slicker as he tried to roll the drover over and get his six-shooter free. Slocum gave up when he realized he would be dead from the bushwhacker's bullets long before he could get his gun free from the dead man.

He dived for cover, hot lead ripping through the air, the reports mingling with the claps of thunder from the storm.

12

Slocum lay flat on his belly, wondering when the slug that would rip his guts out would come through the rain. It didn't come. He wiggled forward in the mud, scrambling to get under the boardwalk. He heard the thunder. His vision blurred slightly when lightning blinded him. But try as he might, he couldn't see where the hidden sniper was.

The rain came down in torrents, heavy white wet curtains blotting out his view. He wiped the mud and water from his eyes. Not five feet away Frank McKenzie lay dead. Slocum considered his chances. Could he get back to the fallen man, roll him over, and retrieve his pistol before getting his head blown off? It didn't seem likely. The sniper could see him far better than he could see the hidden bushwhacker. Even worse, the sharp bass reports meant that the sniper was using a heavy rifle. A .32-caliber Colt wasn't much use against a long-range weapon.

Heavy footfalls sounded just above his head. Slocum cringed down away from them in an involuntary move.

"What in tarnation is going on out here? Lem, go see to that man laying out in the street."

Slocum heard a six-shooter being cocked. Marshal Lewis stood above him, pistol ready to fire at anything moving.

"He's deader'n ary a doornail, Marshal," came the deputy's words. "Shot square in the center of the chest. Reckon it killed him outright. Never knew what happened."

"No need to fetch Doc Pendleton, then." Lewis's boots spattered mud on Slocum as he jumped down from the boardwalk and went into the street. "You see any sign of the varmint who did this?"

"You meanin' that Slocum fella we had in jail?"

Lewis grunted as he bent to examine McKenzie. "Can't see how he did it with his Colt still in the victim's belt." Lewis turned slowly, pistol still in his hand. He looked squarely into Slocum's green eyes. "You come on out now, son. The shootin's over for the time being."

Slocum rolled over and got out from under the walk. He got to his feet and stood staring down at the fallen drover.

"Lem here thinks you had something to do with it. That right?"

"From the report, he was shot with a rifle. All I had to do with it was not being able to get my six-shooter free in time to return fire."

"And where would you have been shootin'?"

Slocum looked up. The rain beat into his face. "That direction. McKenzie was facing that way when he was hit." He bent and pulled his Colt free. Marshal Lewis didn't move to stop him. Slocum checked it to be sure the mud and rain hadn't damaged it, then tucked it away in his holster. Only then did he start walking in the direction of the shots.

Wind whipped blinding sheets of rain back and forth

until Slocum wondered if he would ever be dry. A rueful half smile came to his lips when he realized how lucky he was. Better to be cold and wet and complaining about it than dead, like Frank McKenzie.

He studied the buildings near where the shots had come from. He decided on a two-story brick building and went inside. Clerks with eyeshades and ink guards on their sleeves looked up. A nervous teller in a cage reached under the counter.

"Don't get your dander up, Nels," called out Marshal Lewis. "This ain't a stickup. We want to get up to the second floor and look around."

"That's Mr. Dykstra's office up there," the teller said. "It's not right to go bargin' in on him without announcin' yourself first."

"It's all right, Nels," repeated the marshal, as if soothing a small child. He followed Slocum up the narrow stairs. Slocum studied the lush, deep-pile carpet on the risers and knew they wouldn't find anything up here. Damp footprints leading down showed someone had been out in the rain, hurried up, spent damned little time on the second floor, then rushed back downstairs. If he had been inside the bank building for very long, his boots would have dried.

Slocum paused, then chose the door leading to McCoy and Associates. He kicked the door open. The suite of offices was deserted. He went toward the front of the building and stood by the window. It had been raised six inches, and a steady stream of rain was coming in. On the sill were fresh nicks where a rifle had rested, its metal barrel cutting into the softer wood.

"Reckon it's plain where the son of a bitch shot from," said Marshal Lewis. "It's also as plain as the nose on my face that he's long gone." Without another word, the marshal spun and stalked down the stairs. Slocum stood for a moment, staring at the luxuriously furnished office. Then he followed the lawman to the bank lobby.

"You say you didn't see anyone carrying a rifle come this way?" Lewis demanded of the teller. The man's eyes grew wider than saucers as he shook his head. His pale face turned pasty white.

"I didn't see anything, Marshal. Believe me."

Lewis looked around. The others shook their heads.

"He might have gone out the side door," offered Nels. "We usually keep it locked, but with the rain and all, we thought folks might find it convenient to come in that way. None of us could see anyone coming or going if they used that door."

Slocum checked on it and found that the teller was speaking the truth. The stairs led into a short hallway that went to the side of the bank. A careful man could have made his escape out that door and no one in the bank lobby would have spotted him.

That didn't make McKenzie's death any easier to swallow.

"Who's got access to McCoy's office upstairs?" asked Lewis.

"Well, Mr. McCoy, but he's back east. Then there's Mr. Dykstra and his two clerks."

"Where are the clerks?" cut in Slocum.

"Reckon they stepped out for . . . for a few minutes," the teller finished lamely.

"You mean they went over to the saloon for a little nip, don't you, Nels?"

"I hate to say it, Marshal, but they're both partaking a bit too much of the bottle for my taste. They get boisterous upstairs, and we've had bank customers complain about the noise."

"Reckon that'll be all for now, Nels. Thanks for your help." Lewis took off his hat and wiped the grosgrain ribbon hatband clean of moisture. He finished the small chore, then looked up at Slocum.

"What are you going to do about this, Marshal?" Slocum saw the answer in the man's tired eyes before he heard the answer over the noise of the storm outside.

"Done most all I can do. Anybody could have snuck up there, and nobody here in the bank would know."

"It was Trumble."

"Might have been. Where's the proof?"

"Who else could it have been?"

Lewis snorted and put his hat back on. "Son, you got a powerful lot to learn about city folks. There's dozens— hundreds!—in Abilene who are convinced that McKenzie's longhorns are carrying Texas fever. They'd as soon shoot the drover as the cattle. The fever scares them *that* much." Lewis held up his hand to shut off Slocum's protest. "Trumble might have good cause. I can't say. Fact is, all I got is your word he was even over at Grove's Store."

"They're scared of him. Cameron will tell you."

"Mr. Cameron is scared shitless of his own shadow. I'm not real sure I'd believe him, even if he did tell me. He's got a reputation in these parts of being the one to tell tall tales."

"He wouldn't lie about a thing like that."

"What I'm sayin', son, is that he sometimes can't help himself. He makes things up 'cuz they sound better'n the truth." Lewis heaved another sigh. "There's no way I could track whoever left the upstairs office, not in this rain. Wouldn't trust anyone who could identify a man he saw in this downpour, either."

"So you're not going to do anything?" Slocum held back the cold anger mounting inside him. He wanted to strike out but knew it would do no good to pick a fight with the marshal.

"Heaven alone knows why, but I've taken a liking to you, son. Let me give you some real friendly advice. You go on back to where you got the herd, talk with the cowboys, and you decide what you're going to do now that your boss is dead." Lewis straightened and rested his hand on his well-used six-shooter. "Whatever you all decide, it had better not be ridin' back into Abilene."

"You're chasing us off?"

"I'm keepin' the peace. That's my job, and I take it real serious."

Slocum said nothing about Frank McKenzie appreciating that devotion. His anger turned him even colder inside. The marshal might not be able to do anything—and Slocum saw where there was damned little the lawman could do—but following the strict letter of the law wasn't the only way to see justice done.

"Slocum!" Lewis's voice cut like a knife. "Don't go doing anything you'll regret."

Slocum walked off through the rain, hardly noticing it. Abilene had not been good to him—and he didn't even want to think about what the town had done to Frank McKenzie.

"I reckon there's not a whole lot else we can do," said Kelly. The man scratched his stubbled chin and worked on fixing a smoke. He licked the glue and expertly turned the paper into a cigarette.

Bokemper stretched back on his bedroll, staring up into the ever-changing storm clouds. The rain had stopped, leaving the ground soggy and dangerous, but the new fluffy clouds scudding in from the west promised another downpour before midnight. The burly man propped himself up on one elbow and stared into the fire. It took him some time before he spoke.

"I worked as foreman for Mr. McKenzie for almost a year. This is about the damnedest mess I ever heard of. I ain't got any notion what to do. The herd doesn't belong to any of us."

"We can't drive the longhorns back," added Kelly. "I'm

with you. I don't know what in the hell we're supposed to do. I'd say get out of here, 'cepting we ain't been paid.

Slocum heard the rest of the cowboys grumble and talk among themselves on this point. Like the others, he hated to lose three months' wages. If the herd wasn't sold, none of them would ever see his pay.

"We don't have the right to sign legal papers for Mr. McKenzie," he said, "but that doesn't mean we can't telegraph back to the ranch and get permission."

"That good-for-nothing son of his wouldn't even ride with us," complained Bokemper. "Mr. McKenzie, he always promised me a section of land and a few good breedin' cows when he decided to hang up his spurs."

"None of us are gettin' squat now," bitched another cowboy, sitting just outside the circle of light cast by the campfire. "I say we try to sell the herd for what we can, split the money among ourselves, and then get out of here."

"Who'd buy cows we ain't got fair claim to?" asked Bokemper.

"You're foreman. You're able to act as Mr. McKenzie's agent. You sign, then you pay us what's due. It's only fair." Kelly thought this settled everything.

Slocum didn't even try arguing. He knew it would be damned near impossible to find a buyer now, even if it hadn't been before. The splenic fever scare had many of the townspeople afraid of the longhorns. Not being able to give assurance of ownership of the cattle would scotch any possible dealing.

Slocum rocked back, thinking hard. He owed Frank McKenzie nothing now that the man was dead. He didn't have a wife back in Texas, and Bokemper was right about McKenzie's good-for-nothing son. Sixty dollars in wages were owed, and he might never see it unless they did something.

Coldness formed and spread in his belly when he

thought that Dykstra might now be willing to buy the cattle for a few cents on the dollar of true worth. The cowboys might walk off with their pay and nothing else, but they hadn't expected more than that when they'd signed on for the long, hard drive north.

It offended his sense of duty to think of Dykstra profiting so handsomely when his henchman had been the one to gun down McKenzie. And it was no fault of his that Gus had missed when he had tried to drygulch Slocum outside the Osage reservation.

"Then it's decided," said Bokemper. "We'll mosey on into town tomorrow and see what can be done about getting rid of them damned longhorns." The others agreed. Slocum pulled out his bedroll and tried not to think too much about what might happen. He had been through enough for one day.

"I don't rightly understand what's goin' on here," said Bokemper. The man held his hat in his hand, nervously twisting it around until Slocum thought he might poke holes in the felt. "You say the judge is goin' to decide it?"

"That's the way it looks," said Marshal Lewis. "The townspeople got up a petition to let the judge pass on it."

"It's not up to him," said Slocum. "The herd belongs to McKenzie's heir."

"Then why in the bloody hell is *he* trying to find a buyer for the herd?" Lewis glared at Bokemper.

"He's the foreman. He's acting as McKenzie's son's agent, just as he acted for Mr. McKenzie when he was alive."

"Judge Tellerman isn't going to like this none," said the marshal, shaking his head. "You muddy the waters, you get him madder'n 'ary a wet hen."

The marshal stalked off in the direction of the two-story whitewashed clapboard courthouse. Slocum almost decided to get on his horse and ride off. Once the lawyers got to fighting over the longhorns, nobody would come out a winner—except the lawyers. Still, he had money due him, and he wasn't going to lose it.

"I don't like this much, Slocum," said Bokemper. "What's this judge got to rule on? Nobody's broke the law."

"Let's see." They trailed after the marshal, getting into court just as Judge Tellerman took the bench. The man's hair had turned prematurely gray. For all the shock of gray hair, Slocum guessed the judge couldn't be much over thirty. A few light pink scars crossed his cheeks and chin, making it look as if he had walked through a cobweb.

Tellerman brought his gavel down smartly and bellowed, "Court's in session. You in the back of the room, sit down and shut your mouths or I'll have you evicted." He settled his judicial robes and stared at a stack of papers in front of him. "What is all this?" he asked, looking up.

A man as thin as a rail stood, locked his thumbs in his lapels, and reared back.

"Who's that? He's so bucktoothed, he could eat corn on the cob through a picket fence." Bokemper shifted uneasily on the hard bench at the rear of the courtroom.

"Reckon he's a lawyer," said Slocum. "The question is, who's he representing?"

"Your Honor," the skinny lawyer started, "I represent the firm of Joseph McCoy and Company in this matter."

"You ever represent anybody else, Ralph?" The judge fumbled under his robes and pulled out a silver flask. He unscrewed the cap and took a quick nip.

"Judge Tellerman, I am on retainer and—"

"Can it, Ralph. I got other business to tend to. Say your piece and let's get this over."

"Yes, Your Honor." The lawyer glanced at papers scattered over the table in front of him, then said, "Dr. Pendleton has examined the longhorns in question and has found them contaminated. They are, each and every one, diseased. There is some fear on our expert's part that these longhorns might become carriers and spread the splenic fever."

"What?" Bokemper shot to his feet. "You can't be talkin' about *my* beeves! They're as healthy as I am!"

"Order!" Tellerman slammed his gavel three times. When Bokemper continued to protest loudly, the judge reached under his robes and pulled out a Colt. He cocked it and discharged a single shot. Plaster lath showered from the damaged ceiling. "Another outbreak like that and I'll blow a goddamn hole in your head."

"Your Honor," the lawyer continued smoothly, "these gentlemen are part of the crew responsible for driving the diseased animals into our area."

"Noted," said Tellerman. "You sayin' these longhorns have to be destroyed?"

"The good doctor believes that is the only safe way to protect the citizens of Abilene."

"The beeves are clean!"

"Marshal, blow this man's balls off if he opens his mouth again," ordered Judge Tellerman. "I told you, no more outbursts—and I mean it!" He glared at Bokemper.

Slocum pulled the man back to his seat and whispered, "Let them have their say. We'll be allowed to talk in a few minutes."

"The longhorns aren't sick!"

Slocum roughly jerked at Bokemper's sleeve when the foreman tried one last time to protest. Only after the lawyer had said his piece did Slocum stand.

"Your Honor?"

"You one of the cowboys?" Tellerman glanced in Marshal Lewis's direction and saw the lawman nod. "You got one minute to convince me not to order the cows slaughtered for the good of the community."

"There's no hint of sickness in the cattle," said Slocum. "Pendleton hasn't even *seen* them. There's no way he can pass medical judgment from town."

"Dr. Pendleton is not available for comment," spoke up the lawyer. "His reputation is well known to the court."

"He fixed my gout real good," Tellerman said, taking another swig from his flask. "Whether he knows shit about Texas fever is something else."

"All we want to do is sell the herd and—" Slocum was cut off by the judge rapping the butt of his pistol on the bench.

"That's out of order. Who's got custody of the beeves isn't the issue. If they are sick and diseased is what we're talkin' about here."

"The longhorns are free of any disease, Texas fever or anything else," Slocum said, trying to sound as convincing as possible.

"Your Honor, may I have a moment of your valuable time?" A large man seated in the corner of the room rose. From the flashy brocade vest, the expensive June-bug-colored linen jacket, and the gold chains swinging across his pot belly, Slocum knew him instantly. This was the fat man they'd seen in the bank when McKenzie had tried to get a loan.

"What's eatin' you, Mr. Hammerschmidt?" asked the judge.

Slocum tensed. Josiah Hammerschmidt, the architect of all his troubles, smiled benignly and looked the world like a Dutch uncle. But Trumble worked for the railroad magnate—and whatever land grab was going on had been masterminded by him.

"There is no question in my mind that the cattle must be destroyed."

"You've seen 'em?"

"I have, Your Honor. As you well know, the Kansas Pacific Railroad has shipped thousands of head to Chicago over the past few years. I *know* Texas fever in a cow when I see it."

"That's good enough for me. Destroy the whole damned

herd." Judge Tellerman rapped his pistol smartly, then reversed it and pointed it directly at Bokemper. "You got any trouble with my decision, cowboy?"

"We ain't been paid! We're owed three months' wages!" shouted Bokemper.

"That's a civil matter. File suit."

"McKenzie's dead!"

"Sue his estate."

"Your Honor, a moment," Hammerschmidt cut in smoothly. "I might have a partial remedy for this poor man's problem." Tellerman shrugged and motioned for Hammerschmidt to continue. "The herd must be destroyed. That is a good and wise ruling. However, none of my men are willing to be around infected cattle. I am willing to pay these cowboys, who have ridden with the longhorns for almost three months, the sum of twenty-five dollars each to load the cattle onto cars in the rail yard."

"What are you going to do then?" asked Tellerman.

"The herd will be taken far from Abilene before being destroyed. We have pits dug outside Ellsworth. The longhorns will be shot, put in the pit, and buried."

"Ought to burn 'em," suggested Tellerman. "That'll get rid of the fever once and for all time."

"Consider it done, Your Honor."

"Wait a goldanged minute!" Bokemper shot to his feet, jerking free of Slocum's restraining hand. "I'm owed a hundred and ten dollars. I worked as foreman on the drive."

"I feel my offer of twenty-five dollars—in *gold*—is quite generous," Hammerschmidt said smoothly. "And of course the foreman deserves to be paid more."

Bokemper quieted down. Slocum watched in wonder as Judge Tellerman wrote out the order. Everyone in the court cooperated as if they were pieces of a well-oiled machine.

The shyster lawyer set up the judge. Tellerman waited for Hammerschmidt to make his "generous offer," and the few onlookers representing the town's interests all seemed to think justice had been served.

Abilene was rid of diseased cattle. The cowboys would get a portion of their pay, in gold, and that'd keep them from getting too rowdy. And Slocum had no doubt that the longhorns, once aboard Hammerschmidt's cattle cars, would be on their way to Chicago for sale and slaughter rather than to Ellsworth for destruction.

Josiah Hammerschmidt stood to make a huge fortune out of a tiny investment.

Slocum watched the railroad man huff and puff and talk with the lawyer to work out the details. Hammerschmidt had made a small investment—and taken McKenzie's life. What else was he guilty of? Slocum began to wonder.

13

"Hate to see Mr. McKenzie's beeves killed like this," said Bokemper. The ruddy-faced man took off his Stetson and wiped the sweat off his face. The longhorns protested loudly as the cowboys drove them toward the railhead. Keeping a sharp eye on them were several of Josiah Hammerschmidt's men, and rocked back in a chair in the cool shade over by the main office sat Lem Washington, the deputy. Beside him rested his shotgun.

Slocum didn't answer directly. Bokemper still hadn't twigged to Hammerschmidt's real motives. The only thing any of the cowboys could think about was the twenty-five dollars gold they'd been promised. In their eyes, this made the railroad director purt-near the most generous man on Earth. One minute, their employer had lain murdered in a muddy Abilene street and the beeves were a liabilty—and they had no prospect for recovering any of their wages.

The next instant they got almost half of what was due them. It didn't really matter that Hammerschmidt would become rich off this single herd. Slocum snorted and shook his head. Hammerschmidt was paying only five hundred dollars for damned near twenty-eight hundred longhorns going for thirty a head, easy.

Bokemper and the others ignored this; they believed that the cattle would be taken away toward Ellsworth and destroyed to rid the countryside of the nonexistent splenic fever contamination.

"That's about got 'em all rounded up, Bo," called Lucas Kelly. The man's leathery face was grimy with sweat and streaked with dirt, but his broken-toothed smile shone through. They were at the end of the trail, and that was all that counted.

"Good enough. Let's go talk to Mr. Hammerschmidt's agent about getting our money."

Slocum had to quiet his horse when the train whistle blew. The long freight train laden with the cattle began to move slowly. In less than a minute it had built up enough power to move the cars. In ten the train had vanished from sight. Only a column of white smoke rose in the distance to mark the locomotive's progress toward—where?

Slocum guessed Hammerschmidt would take the cattle to Chicago. He might consider stopping before then. St. Louis would be the next best choice, but considering how the beeves had been obtained, the huge markets of Chicago would swallow the cattle without a trace.

The rich got richer. Slocum fumed a bit at this. He was out a full thirty-five dollars for his work over the past three months.

And Frank McKenzie was dead.

He dismounted after the others had gathered at the depot. He saw Dykstra talking in low tones to the lawyer who had convinced the judge to "destroy" the beeves. The scrawny shyster bobbed his head up and down like a feather caught in a tornado. Whatever he was arguing with Dykstra about, the lawyer wasn't getting the best of it and showed it.

He stomped over. "Men, you've done good work for Mr. Hammerschmidt—and the community of Abilene. Those diseased animals are better off being put out of their misery." Some grumbling about their being healthy Texas longhorns went through the crowd of cowboys but quickly died down. "Mr. Hammerschmidt is so pleased with your hard work and devotion to upholding the lawful execution of the court order, he's authorized another . . . five dollars each."

Dykstra's expression showed extreme disapproval. Slocum wondered if the cattleman's agent had wanted to pocket this small bit of extra money and to hell with the cowboys. The skinny lawyer seemed willing to buy some peace of mind and leave everyone sure that Josiah Hammerschmidt was the most generous man alive. A night's revelry would take most of the thirty dollars, and then the trail-weary cowhands would drift out of town looking for work elsewhere and not be seen again in Abilene this year.

Slocum's thoughts turned away from the speech the lawyer was inflicting on the cowboys before he dispensed their money. Trumble still rode the range scot-free. And then there was Claire. He ought to go out to her farm and talk with her before he rode off.

That thought worked away at him. Should he ride off and abandon such a fine-looking woman? She'd had a run of bad luck. It hadn't been any of her doing that her husband had gotten hooked by a longhorn and died on his wedding day. She had come out to Kansas to live the life of a farmer's wife and had ended up with dirt—less.

"Slocum, wake up. Go get your wages." Bokemper nudged him again to make sure he was awake. Slocum pushed through the crowd and accepted his pay for the day's work. The double eagle and the slim gold coins rounded out the thirty dollars due him.

It felt like blood money. Hammerschmidt and the emaciated lawyer and Dykstra were buying off McKenzie's riders. That's the only reason the railroad magnate was willing to be so "generous."

"Let's go get drunk," shouted Kelly. "Then let's get laid!" The others joined in a long, loud cheer. In less than a minute, only a dust cloud marked where they had been.

"You comin', Slocum?" asked Bokemper. "Hell man, *I'll* buy the first one. Then you're on your own."

"How can I pass up an offer like that?" Slocum swung into the saddle. The deputy had already returned to other business. Dykstra and the lawyer were still arguing but had come to a guarded truce, with only occasional noisy outbursts. Slocum found he really didn't care anymore. A tiredness descended over him just like the twilight settled over the prairie and hid the bright light of day.

The notion of getting roaring drunk appealed to him more and more.

The Longhorn Saloon had been a powerful magnet drawing the thirsty cowboys. They had ridden by the flashier Alamo, though the name did provoke a few crude comments about Mexicans and making a last stand. The Longhorn had been decked out in such a fashion that there wasn't too much breakable around. Ankle-deep sawdust on the floor muffled the sounds of half a hundred rowdy patrons stomping about—and the infrequent one being knocked down or falling over drunk. Most of all, the pictures of nudes hanging high up on the walls drew the cowboys' loud and frequent appreciation.

Slocum had several drinks and saw where the night was heading. Whores drifted in alone and left with partners, only to return in a few minutes. He reckoned their customers—or victims—would wake up with a splitting head and one whale of a story to tell to anyone who'd listen.

The whiskey tasted bitter on his tongue. He didn't even sample the fourth setup in front of him. He just wasn't in the mood to get drunk. Slocum turned and looked at the men in the saloon. He had lived with them for three months, sharing the trail and dangers and the eventual disaster in Abilene. Most drovers died along the trail. Few were gunned down trying to sell their herds.

He ought to feel more toward these men. He didn't. He spun and left the saloon without another look. The ride out of Abilene started as aimless drifting but ended up a beeline for Claire Carson's farm. Dogs yelped and barked as he rode past the farm where the sodbusters had offered the cowboys a cool drink and some friendship. He rode past, cutting across plowed, weeded fields that might belong to the half-crazy, rusty-gun-toting Cameron, then down into the rangelands where poorly tended land marked the start of Claire's spread.

Slocum reined in when he got within hailing distance. Indecision washed over him like waves working on a shoreline. One second he wanted to ride down, yelling and whooping and calling for Claire. In the next, he wanted to turn and ride west. Something out there would appeal to him. Something just over the horizon beckoned.

A gunshot decided him. Slocum put his heels into the horse's sides and raced for the sod farmhouse. He hit the ground while the horse was still putting its hooves into the soft dirt.

"Claire!" he called. "Where are you?"

A second gunshot came from the direction of the chicken coop. Slocum drew his Colt and got himself under tighter rein. Rushing into the middle of a gunfight would only get him killed. If he wanted to come out with his hide in one piece, he had to be more cautious—but the notion of Claire being in danger pushed him toward recklessness.

"Quiet, you two-bit whore!" The words rang out in the

stillness of the night. A loud *smack!* sounded. Slocum
mentally pictured a heavy palm slapping Claire. He cocked
his Colt and pressed against the back of the henhouse.
Through a crack in the boards he saw Claire cringing
down. On either side of her stood two men, their backs to
Slocum.

He circled the coop, saw a pair of horses tethered over
by the pigsty and decided these were the only two he had to
deal with.

"Sign the damned papers and be done with it. You
won't get a better offer," spoke up the second man, his
voice grating and harsh.

"We might give you somethin' special if'n you don't
raise any more of a ruckus."

"If I don't legally own the land, why do I have to sign
anything?" Claire sounded scared, but Slocum heard the
edge of courage cutting through the words.

"Do as you're told. We want this to be legal all around.
You ain't got claim to the land, not with your husband
dead. But we want to be damned sure no one questions
this."

Slocum held back when he heard the man slap Claire
again. She let out a tiny whimper, but her voice didn't
quaver. "Go to hell. I'm not signing anything!"

Slocum knew the men's attention would be on Claire.
He swung around, got his bearings, and fired. The first
shot took the man slapping Claire high in the shoulder. The
other jerked in reaction to the Colt's sharp report; Slocum
missed him by inches.

"John!"

"Get down!" he ordered. Lead started flying, and he
wasn't sure where it came from or went.

Slocum fired twice more. From the moan of pain, he
guessed he had finished off the man he had winged. The
second owlhoot moved too fast for him, though. A snap-
ping noise from the rear of the chicken coop told him that

the man had kicked out part of the wall. Slocum hurried around, paying no attention to Claire's cries for help. The best way he could help her was to put the other gunman six feet under.

Two shots took off his hat. Slocum ducked, weaved, and feinted to the left. As he dived right, he saw a long orange tongue of flame betraying the outlaw's position. Slocum aimed and fired his last two rounds straight for the flare.

He cursed when he heard nothing. Fumbling, he got his Colt reloaded. Every second he wasted gave his opponent that much more time to work his deadly mischief.

Colt charged again, Slocum wiggled forward on his belly, ignoring the mixture of dust and mud. He wouldn't have believed it had rained torrentially within the past day from the way the dirt had dried out. He kicked himself into a roll and came to his feet behind the tethered horses. If the would-be killer wanted to get out of here, he had to get to his horse.

Slocum strained to hear the slightest sounds in the night. Claire sobbed uncontrollably in the chicken coop. The horses pawed and snuffled and rattled their bridles impatiently. In the distance he heard a wolf howling, and the wind slipped softly through the grass, making whispering noises.

Of the gunman he heard nothing.

Slocum went exploring. On feet as light as any cat, he moved shadowlike toward the spot where he had last sighted his foe. Careful as he was, Slocum almost tripped over the body. He bent and examined the corpse. Both shots had caught the man high in the middle of his chest, blasting apart windpipe and throat. From the look of the wounds, he had drowned in his own blood, unable to call out.

Slocum lowered the hammer on his six-shooter and holstered it. He heaved a deep sigh. The fight was over. For now. He went back to the coop, not knowing what to expect. He didn't think they had hurt Claire too bad. Scared the hell out her, maybe, but nothing more.

"John, you're safe!" She threw her arms around his neck and buried her face in his shoulder. Shudders wracked her body, but he didn't feel any tears on his shirt. She had gone beyond that. "They came and demanded that I give them the farm."

"Come on back to the house. It's all over. They're both dead."

"They wanted the land. Why did they me to sign anything? You said the land wasn't really mine, that it belonged to Benjamin."

She started to babble. Slocum supported her with an arm around her waist until they got to the sod house. He didn't bother listening to her. His mind raced to cover the angles. He had never seen the two men before, but there weren't too many players in this deadly game. They had to work for Josiah Hammerschmidt. Who else benefited from owning this land?

If the railroad director got control of this land, he had prime grazing land for cattle driven up from Texas and the right-of-way for a spur line to the Kansas Pacific railhead. Such a combination might breathe life back into Abilene as a cow town—and make Hammerschmidt fabulously wealthy. Dodge City and Ellsworth and Wichita had started getting the bulk of the longhorns. Even Caldwell, which had never amounted to a hill of beans, took away valuable business from Abilene.

Slocum snorted in disgust. Even if Hammerschmidt's land grab didn't work, he had done right fine by himself stealing Frank McKenzie's herd.

"They'll be back, won't they? Not them. You said they were dead. But others. They're going to keep coming, aren't they?"

"I'll see what can be done to stop them," Slocum said.

"I need a husband. I need a man who can file the claim deed to the farm, and they won't be able to argue with that." She looked up, her blue eyes dry and bright.

He didn't bother telling her that a man as powerful as Hammerschmidt could hire lawyers to make any claim invalid. The railroad magnate had dealt fairly with the Osage Indians in obtaining their land only because any dispute there might bring in the U.S. Cavalry.

"You saved my life," Claire said. She turned in the circle of his arms, her body pressed warmly against his. She closed her eyes slowly, tilted her head back, and pursed her lips. Slocum bent down and lightly kissed her. Claire wanted nothing of that. Her arms tightened like steel bands, pulling him even closer. Her lips crushed his with passion.

They turned slightly and sat down on the small bed. Slocum had seen a sleight-of-hand magician in a traveling medicine show once. He had pulled cards out of thin air and made coins taken from the audience disappear. Claire worked even more effective magic. She made their clothes disappear and never once did she break off their deep kiss.

"Claire," he said, trying to speak.

"Make love to me. I need it, John. After all that's happened, I need it. I need you!"

Her weight carried him down to the bed. Her breasts flattened as she pressed down atop him. Her lips worked eagerly against his, then began slipping down, to his chest, to his belly, lower. Slocum gasped as her lips closed around his throbbing manhood. Her fingers worked on his hairy balls even as her lips kissed and excited him.

She lingered for a few minutes, then slid back up his body. They kissed once more, Slocum rolling over. The woman's legs parted eagerly for him.

"Hurry, John. I can't stand it without you inside me. Hurry!" Her fingernails raked his back. Even if he tried to escape—even if he had *wanted* to—he was trapped in the circle of her arms.

He stroked along her inner thighs, getting her legs spread even more. The head of his hot shaft touched her nether lips. They both trembled now. He moved another inch forward. Moisture and sultry heat circled his length. He slipped fully into her yearning interior.

The dark-haired woman sobbed and arched her back, lifting her ass off the bed. She began grinding her crotch into his, stirring their desires to the breaking point.

Slocum pulled back, then slowly dived back in. He found his control slipping. Her obvious need for him pushed him quickly to the point of no return. His hips swung back and forth, faster, more insistent. Claire gasped and moaned and kissed, her head tossing on the thin feather pillow. Her hands stroked along his sides, then cupped his behind. She started pulling him into her.

A burning tide rose within him that he could not deny. He got harder. He stroked with the ages-old rhythm of a man loving a woman. Then it was over. He shot his wad so fast that it felt as if he hadn't had a woman for months. Slocum sagged onto Claire. She breathed warmly in his ear, her hands stroking gently over his broad back. He rolled to one side, wanting to talk to her.

The lovemaking had been the release of tension the woman needed. She slept peacefully, an angelic expression on her face. Slocum wasn't about to wake her to say what had to be said.

He lay beside her for some time before drifting off to a troubled sleep.

14

John Slocum got out of bed long before sunup. He dressed, not caring if he woke Claire. She didn't stir, even when he sat down at the small table, tore apart his Colt, cleaned it, and reassembled it, fully loaded. He glanced over at her. She lay with a hint of a smile on her lips, her hair spread over the pillow like a dark halo.

Slocum climbed the steps to the outdoors and shivered as a sudden breeze came whipping across the prairie. The wind was hot and humid; he reacted to the tension in the air. Another thunderstorm would be pelting the landscape with heavy droplets within the hour. The air carried a heavy garlic odor from lightning he saw in the distance but couldn't hear.

Finding a shovel, he went out to the chicken coop. The hens were still roosting, hunched down in feathery masses. Some slept with their heads under their wings. Slocum envied them this ability. He wished he could turn his back to the troubles all around him—but he couldn't.

He dragged the first gunman he'd shot up the slight slope and stopped, wondering if he should bury him next to Benjamin Carson. It seemed a travesty. Then he began digging in the hard ground. Cemeteries didn't sort out their residents. One dead man didn't care who the one in the next grave was—or had been.

Slocum got the second gunman buried just before the rains started. He rushed to the chicken coop and disturbed a few of the fowl. They squawked sleepily, then returned to their dreams of roosters and brown-speckled eggs. He fished out the papers he had taken from the dead men and spread them out on the floor to read.

By the flashes of lightning that danced overhead, he made out the papers. They'd been drawn up all legal and proper, naming Ralph Snodgrass as new owner. Slocum frowned. The name wasn't familiar. Then it dawned on him. The skinny lawyer representing Dykstra in court had been called Ralph by the judge. There weren't many in Kansas who might be pulling such a land swindle. Lawyer Ralph had to be the man named as new owner of the homestead land.

Slocum didn't miss the way the document had been dated just before Carson's death—and how a large black X had been entered in the space marked LEGAL SIGNATURE. The two gunmen hadn't wanted Claire to sign the land over. They wanted her to witness her husband's mark.

That made more sense to Slocum. Women couldn't own land. The concept was ridiculous. Homesteads were proved by men and the land given to men if they were successful.

He sat cross-legged on the coop floor and watched the slow march of the summer rainstorm crossing the prairie. The sun wouldn't shine today. Not on this land. Slocum felt cold inside. The sun wouldn't be shining on many of

the homesteaders standing in Hammerschmidt's way, unless the railroad man was stopped.

Slocum thought on it awhile and couldn't decide how to
help Claire or the others. He didn't owe them anything.
But a friend had been gunned down. Whether Trumble had
done it or Hammerschmidt had ordered it didn't much matter. Both were guilty of McKenzie's death. In a crazy way,
Slocum held Hammerschmidt as even guiltier than the man
pulling the trigger. Without Hammerschmidt's brains and
greed, Trumble wouldn't have been inclined to murder the
drover.

Slocum had almost thirty dollars jingling in his pocket.
He had spent a few dollars buying drinks at the Longhorn
Saloon. The notion that he had been cheated out of half the
money due him for his work on the drive rankled too. Josiah Hammerschmidt was the hub of a wheel, and every
spoke led directly to him.

That wheel would have to be spun a mite, Slocum decided. Justice might be slow in coming to a man as wealthy
and powerful as the railroad magnate, but it would come.
His hand touched the ebony handle of his Colt.

It would come, one way or another.

He got up and ran back to the sod house. The rain was
coming down in buckets now, drenching him thoroughly.
He ducked inside and stood, dripping on the dirt floor,
making small puddles. Claire was still asleep. He started to
wake her, then stopped. He turned over the bogus land
deed, found a stick, rubbed it in the soot on the oil lamp's
chimney, and wrote her a quick note explaining that he was
going into town to straighten out matters.

Slocum paused before going back into the rain. She
looked so lovely he didn't want to leave. But he did. Too
many crooked matters were circling around and coming to
rest on Hammerschmidt's doorstep. They'd have to be
taken care of or nobody would know a minute's peace.

His horse hadn't been tended to, but without proper

stables, it didn't mean much to curry the animal in a driving rain. Slocum got out his yellow slicker and put it on. "Old girl," he said, patting the horse's neck, "it'll get a sight worse before it gets better. I promise you some grain when we get to Abilene. It's the least I can do."

The horse turned a chocolate brown eye on him. Accusations flashed there, then the horse bowed her head and heaved a deep sigh. Slocum took this for agreement. He mounted and rode off slowly through the rain, not wanting to hurry. The mud turned slicker than glass. A misstep might cause his horse to break a leg.

The rain never let up all the way into Abilene. Slocum dismounted and led his horse to a livery.

The stable boy came running out, not caring if he got wet. "Take your horse, mister?"

"How much to groom and feed?"

The stable boy eyed the condition of the horse, then said, "Six bits. This is going to take a bit of work."

"Done. And don't let me catch you scrimping on the grain."

"No, sir!" The boy's eyes lit up when Slocum tossed him a shiny silver dollar.

"Any of the hands from the McKenzie drive still around?"

"They've mostly left town by now. Marshal Lewis threatened a couple with jail unless they got out quick. The others got soused up good and proper, then got robbed." The boy shrugged. "You know how it is with whores and all."

Slocum nodded. He hadn't expected much else. All cow towns were alike. The cowboys worked for months and then squandered their earnings in a night of revelry. Then they moved on, looking for work somewhere else so they could repeat the earn-drink-whore-go broke cycle.

"You lookin' for a place to stay?"

"Could be. Haven't decided how long I'm going to be here."

"The owner might not care if you slept in the barn. Wouldn't charge more than . . . fifty cents."

The way the boy said it, Slocum guessed the going rate was half that. The other two bits would end up in this young tycoon's pocket.

"I'll let you know. Get onto that horse, now. I may be back before sundown."

"Hard to tell when that is, what with the rain coming down like this." The tow-headed boy glanced into the storm, then led Slocum's horse back into the stable and began getting the tack off.

Slocum considered going to the marshal's office and telling Lewis all he knew of Hammerschmidt's scheme. It took him less than a second to decide that that would avail him little. Even if Lewis believed every word, what could the marshal do? Hammerschmidt was a rich and powerful man. His scheme might even breathe life back into Abilene, after several years of steady decline. Although the townspeople weren't too fond of the railroad man, this opportunity might change their minds. The promise of money did that to people.

He stopped and stared at the bank building where Joseph McCoy had his second-floor offices. The windows were closed. Slocum hadn't thought they would leave open the window from which McKenzie had been murdered. He walked to the side and tested the door. As before when it had rained, the door was open. He slipped inside.

Making his way carefully down the passage, he knew he wasn't seen by any of the clerks or tellers in the bank lobby. He went up the stairs two steps at a time. The occasional creaking protest as his weight sagged on the risers couldn't be heard over the roar of the wind and rain.

At the top of the stairs, he paused and looked at the three office doors opening off the landing. One was

marked MCCOY AND ASSOCIATES. One had been nailed
shut. The other door carried a neat sign proclaiming
KANSAS ENTERPRISES.

Slocum had no idea what type of business that must be,
but the vagueness drew him. He had been in the other
office. He doubted anything of real importance was left
there—he even doubted Joe McCoy knew how his agent
operated. Dykstra wouldn't be foolish enough to leave incriminating evidence where his employer might find it.

Slocum pressed his ear against the frosted glass in the
Kansas Enterprises door. The rain deadened any sound
from inside. He took a chance and turned the knob slowly.
He smiled when he found it was locked. That meant whoever used this as an office had decided to take the day off.
With the rain pouring down outside, not many business-
men would be eager to venture out.

A quick jerk snapped off the cheap lock on the door.
Slocum had some trouble getting the bolt free, but a little
discreet rattling forced it. He slipped into the darkened
room. The jagged bolts of lightning arching across the sky
gave him enough light to see a large wooden desk and a
pair of file cabinets.

He edged across the room and sat down in a chair behind the desk. He tried the center drawer, looking for some
sign of what business was transacted in this office. The
drawer was locked, as were the others. Slocum took a pen-
knife off the desk and used it to force open the center
drawer.

A quick look at the papers showed who owned Kansas
Enterprises. Josiah Hammerschmidt's name showed up in
enough places to prove that he was owner. Slocum rocked
back and tried to read the documents he had found. None
made much sense. He thrust them back into the drawer and
turned to the file cabinets along the outer wall.

"There's something inside here he wants to protect real
bad," he said to himself. The cabinets had been chained

shut and securely fastened with heavy padlocks.

Getting the chains off without a hacksaw looked to be impossible. Slocum took another tack. He used the tip of the tiny knife to worry a small hole in the wooden cabinet. Ten minutes of work, illuminated by the flashing lightning outside and the rumble of heavy thunder, saw a space large enough for him to get his hand inside.

Pulling out handfuls of paper, he went back to the desk and examined them. Although he suspected these incriminated Hammerschmidt and Dykstra in illegal activities, they were of interest only to Joseph McCoy, who seemed to be on the losing end. That Dykstra was stealing from his boss didn't surprise Slocum. With McCoy back east trying to raise more money to keep his flagging business afloat, Dykstra had a clear shot at theft.

Slocum stuffed these into an envelope he found and addressed it to Joseph McCoy. He would see that the mail delivered the evidence to McCoy. But he needed more. He needed something showing how and why Hammerschmidt sent his henchmen to force the homesteaders like Claire off their land.

Slocum tossed the envelope intended for McCoy to the side so he could work in earnest on the rest of the papers. Another hour of hunting through the files finally paid off. A small tin box in the bottom file drawer contained forged land deeds, plans for the rail spur Hammerschmidt planned, even evidence that he and Dykstra had recently sold beeves in Chicago for a princely sum. Although not identified as such, Slocum knew they had to be McKenzie's longhorns. Slocum sagged back in the chair and turned to watch the storm.

He had the evidence. What would he do with it? Marshal Lewis might be able to act, but nothing in the papers incriminated Hammerschmidt with McKenzie's murder. Trumble had pulled the trigger. Slocum's gut-level feeling on that couldn't be wrong. Only if he got Trumble to confess could he implicate the railroad director.

Even then, Slocum wasn't sure if Hammerschmidt would ever stand trial. He was a rich and influential man. His web of power had to extend far beyond Abilene. Was the governor in his hip pocket? Did the Kansas Pacific Railroad command more influence than even this? Hammerschmidt might be able to get the politicians in Washington to dance to his tune.

Damned carpetbaggers. Damned Reconstruction. Damned greedy influence peddlers—and buyers.

Slocum decided he would be content with getting Hammerschmidt to stop beating up innocent women and frightening homesteaders. There had been a deed in the box showing that Hammerschmidt had legally purchased the Osage land. That had been the last legal thing he had done.

"Somebody's inside!" The alarm from outside brought Slocum around. He had been foolish to simply sit in the chair and watch the storm's progress. He should have taken the evidence and got the hell out of Hammerschmidt's office. Now he was discovered.

"Look'it the carpet," came a second voice. "Damp footprints."

"You jackass. Look at the *door!* Someone's busted the lock."

Slocum slid his pistol from his holster. He stuffed the papers from the file cabinet into his pockets, not caring if they got torn. Getting out alive counted more right now.

The door flew inward as one of the men kicked hard at it. The shattering glass gave Slocum a split second to act. He fired past the man outlined in the doorway and hit the one standing at the top of the stairs. The bullet didn't cause any real damage; Slocum had barely winged the man. But he took a half step back and went tumbling ass over teakettle down the stairs, shouting as he went.

This distracted the man in the doorway long enough for

Slocum to rush him. His Colt rose and fell. The barrel crashed down hard on the man's wrist, causing him to yelp and drop his six-shooter.

"Son of a bitch!" he cried. "I'll bust your head for this!"

Slocum found himself caught up in a bear hug that robbed him of breath. Powerful arms prevented him from bringing his Colt up past his side.

"Got you now, you little sneak thief!"

The burly man jerked and sent the last of the breath Slocum had trapped in his lungs gusting out. The world spun. The lightning crashes outside got farther and farther away. The roaring in his ears built until he knew he was about ready to pass out. With the last of his strength, he tightened his trigger finger. The report was muffled—but the howl of pain from his target wasn't.

He couldn't aim with his arms locked to his sides; he had discharged the pistol into his attacker's fleshy upper thigh. Slocum fell backward and slammed hard against the wall. He sucked in two painful breaths. Enough strength returned for him to raise his six-shooter.

"You're dead if you take another step," Slocum warned. The man had struggled to get to one knee. He clutched his wounded thigh. Thin red trickles of blood oozed around his strong fingers.

"I'll break your neck just like I was wringin' a chicken's neck," the man promised. "You ain't seen the last of me."

"Where's Trumble?" Slocum asked on impulse.

"He's . . ." The wounded glared at Slocum. "You ain't gettin' shit out of me!"

Slocum saw the man who had fallen down the stairs struggling to get back up. Behind him a small crowd was forming. Slocum figured it must be tellers and customers from the bank. He didn't much care who gathered there. The light reflecting off a shotgun barrel convinced him that he wasn't leaving the building by retreating down the stairs.

The bull of a man made a lunge for him while he was

distracted by the crowd. Slocum spun, his pistol coming about in a short, sharp arc. He laid his barrel alongside the man's head hard enough to stun him.

Slocum sprinted back into Hammerschmidt's office and went to the window. One quick heave got the window open. Rain pelted him in the face. Wind whipped the papers scattered on the desk onto the floor. Slocum worried more about the two-story drop. If he slipped in the muddy street when he hit, he'd be a dead man.

Slocum squeezed a round off through the doorway to keep the crowd rushing up at bay. Then he ducked behind the file cabinet he had ransacked.

Bullets flew, and he crouched down even further. He hoped his gamble would pay off. If not, he'd at least die in a dry office instead of ending up face-down in the mud and rain.

A half-dozen men charged into the office. The roar of the shotgun produced cries of outrage.

"Take that damned thing away from Ned 'fore he hurts somebody!" yelled an angry man.

"Get it away from him before he kills *me!*" demanded another.

"Where'd he go?"

Slocum stood and moved to the edge of the crowd still forcing its way into the office. "Out the window. He went out the window and down into the street. I saw him!"

Several rushed over. One whipped out a derringer and loosed a round into the storm. "Damn, missed him."

"After him!" someone else called.

"Get him," Slocum added, yelling with the rest. He moved closer to two other men wearing slickers. Neither of the men who had discovered him in the office were likely to identify him. The one he'd pistol-whipped lay flat on his back, still unconscious. The other had never gotten a good look at him.

With the crowd intent on tearing the fleeing sneak thief

limb from limb, Slocum ran into the bank lobby.

Slocum hung back when Marshal Lewis burst in and demanded to know what was going on. Slocum pressed against a wall as the marshal went by and up the stairs with Hammerschmidt's henchman.

From the top of the stairs, he heard the marshal shout, "I'll have the ears of anyone going after the robber. That's *my* job, damnit!"

Slocum exchanged a few words of false concern with others in the bank. Only after Lewis had left to hunt down the fleeing sneak thief did Slocum leave the bank.

He had proof of Hammerschmidt's crimes. But what was he going to do with it now? Even worse, he would eventually end up a suspect for the robbery, just because he was a cowboy. He smiled crookedly. The man who had tried to mash him like a bug with the bear hug might even be able to identify him.

It wouldn't hurt to blow town, he decided, until this storm passed. In the meantime, he could decide what to do with the incriminating documents stuffed into his pockets.

15

Slocum licked his lips and tasted blood. When the mountain of a man had tried to crush him, he had bitten himself. He spat, the bloody froth floating away in the rain. Slocum stuck his face up to the rain and let the pure, clean, warm water wash over him. It wasn't the same as a real scrubbing, but it would do for the time being.

He shook himself as dry as he could get in the rain and walked slowly down the boardwalk toward the saloons. Stopping in front of the Drover's House, he knew that was a bad idea. Throughout Abilene bands of men were patrolling the streets looking for him.

Slocum knew that only the one could identify him, but vigilantes didn't care about truth. The idea of finding someone to string up gave their dull lives a moment's excitement. Guilty or innocent didn't much matter to a man with an itchy trigger finger.

He had to admit also that Hammerschmidt's henchmen had a stake in making sure he didn't escape. They had no idea what he might have found in the office. To tell their boss that they had allowed anyone to get such damning evidence might mean their own heads.

The notion of having a drink, as appealing as it was now, would be too dangerous. Slocum sat in a chair in front of the hotel and waited, watching the men running from one end of town to the other. Marshal Lewis and two deputies were trying to restore order. They weren't entirely successful, but they did get a few of the wilder vigilantes off the streets.

This gave Slocum the hope of getting away from Abilene. A few days away from the city might allow him to figure out his best tactic. During the war he had been a sniper and a good one. He had patience others lacked. He could lie quietly on a grassy ridge for hours waiting for the flash of sunlight reflected off a Yankee officer's gold braid. A single shot might cut the head off the enemy. Without officers, the infantry milled around and created confusion.

He knew those tactics. He knew waiting. All Slocum had to do was get away from the center of the storm he had caused and ride it out.

Then he could cut the head off the enemy.

Without hurrying, he made his way back to the stables. The stable boy had finished currying the horse and feeding it. She munched noisily on the oats the boy had given her. Slocum hated to pull the horse away from the first good meal she'd had in weeks, but he'd hate even more to run afoul of Hammerschmidt's gunmen.

"She ready to ride?" he called out. The stable hand looked up from a newspaper. It took several seconds for him to leave behind the world of print and figure out what was going on.

"You sure ain't givin' her much of a rest, mister."

"Get on back to your reading," Slocum said. It was rare

finding a stable boy who followed town gossip like this. "I'll be back in an hour or so." That was a lie, but it put the boy's mind to rest.

Slocum saddled the protesting horse, patted her, and found a carrot in a nearby bin to give as a peace offering. The horse accepted it reluctantly, knowing rain and mud would soon follow.

Slocum ducked as he went through the barn door and out into the driving rain. He'd never seen this much rain fall in such a short time. He knew the farmers enjoyed rain, but too much washed away crops and topsoil. To replant this late in the growing season would mean stunted crops come fall and a poor harvest price.

That might play into Josiah Hammerschmidt's hands too. The railroad director might be able to buy up even more of the homesteaders' land for his new railroad spur and fattening pens. Slocum heaved a sigh. From everything he had heard, Joe McCoy had built the cattle trade in Abilene and was an honest man. He could only wonder what McCoy would do if he found his own agent and Hammerschmidt in cahoots to do him out of his cattle brokerage business.

Slocum kept riding slowly, not wanting to look as if he was hurrying, when he saw a half-dozen men coming out of the bank. Standing in the middle of the tight knot of men was the only one who could identify him. The man roared and shouted and carried on. Slocum pulled his hat down over his eyes and lowered his head, as if keeping the rain out of his face.

He kept riding, but he had done something to attract the crowd's attention. He heard a silence fall, then a single, gravelly voice shouted, "Him! He's the son of a bitch I almost kilt upstairs! He's the damned thief!"

Slocum tried to fake his way out by looking around to see who the man meant. It didn't work. Pistols came out from under slickers and began going off—in his direction.

Lead flew like angry bees over his head. He bent low and put his spurs into the horse's flanks. The animal jumped almost straight up at the unexpected and painful urging. Then the horse neighed and dug in her hooves. Mud flew back into the crowd, blinding many. The shots went wild.

"After him! Don't let him get away or Mr. Hammerschmidt will have our hides for it!"

Slocum raced into the storm, not knowing what direction he was traveling in. He hoped that this lack of destination would serve him well. Those hot on his trail might think he was heading for somewhere in particular and go there. All he wanted was to ride in a huge circle and maybe come back into town in a day or two.

The road vanished under him. The rain had washed out huge sections. He crossed railroad tracks twice, then came to a broad, fast-flowing river. It took several seconds for him to realize he had started south, doubled back, and was now west of town, with Mud Creek blocking his path. On the east side of the raging stream, maybe fifteen miles distant, would be Detroit. If he turned due west, Solomon City lay about as far. The only trouble with either destination was that both lay on the Kansas Pacific line. A locomotive could beat him to either by half a day.

If he turned around and headed back south he would have to ford the Smoky River. In this storm, that river would be swollen and overflowing its banks. Even Mud Creek looked well nigh impassable.

The only good thing about riding through such inclement weather was the difficulty in tracking him. The spoor he left behind would be washed away immediately.

He swung to the west and rode until he came to a low, rocky ridge. He urged his horse to the top and dismounted. He tried to get his bearings without providing a good target for lightning strikes. Wiping the rain from his eyes, he saw that he wasn't far from the Osage encampment. Dropping in on the Indians unannounced was not a smart thing to do, but Slocum was getting soaked to the bone. He didn't want the water destroying the papers he had stuffed in his pockets. Without them he could prove nothing against Hammerschmidt.

He didn't bother riding his horse down the sodden slope and into the silent Osage village. By taking his time, he gave them plenty of time to notice that he was coming, that he was alone, and that he had no intention of harming them.

At least Slocum hoped that was the peaceable message they got. If nothing else, his horse thanked him for not forcing her down the treacherously muddy hill.

Slocum stopped a few yards away from the Osage he had spoken to before. "I seek shelter from the rain," he called out.

The Indian he had met before, Buffalo Pizzle, gestured impatiently to him. Slocum heaved a sigh of relief. The Indian accepted him into his village without question—or gunfire. Normal debate might have lasted an hour or more.

"They call me foolish," the Indian said. "I am too much like the round eyes, they say. I am too impatient." The Osage sank to the ground inside a small hut. A cookfire blazed merrily. To Slocum's surprise a pot of coffee was brewing. His nostrils flared with the pungent, inviting aroma.

"You drink coffee?"

"This, too, is like the white man," the Indian said, almost sadly. "I have caught a strange disease. Those who were my friends might be right. I may be changing."

"Change is all around us. The weather does not remain constant. In a few hours, the storm will break and the sun will shine. Why should a brave remain the same?"

"You flee those in Abilene?"

"Why do you ask?" Slocum accepted a battered tin cup of the coffee. It burned his tongue and throat, but he didn't care. Soaked as he was, it warmed him from the inside out.

"Until they move us again, we are imprisoned on this reservation, but we still have ears and eyes. We see many posses riding from the city, seeking someone. You are alone. Can it be you they seek?"

"Buffalo Pizzle is a wise man," Slocum said, his mind racing. He wouldn't lie to the Indian, yet he wanted a few hours' rest. The Osage might provide that.

"You must finish your coffee and leave quickly. We cannot have you found here." The Indian pulled a blanket around his sloping shoulders. "Once we would have been able to fight to protect guests of the tribe. We no longer have the will. Being on the white man's reservation has broken the Osage's spirit."

"You are still strong. You have many fine warriors who are strong." Slocum finished the coffee and put the tin cup down on the dirt floor. "However, fighting to protect one who is no longer a guest of the tribe is pointless."

Buffalo Pizzle's eyebrows arched slightly. "You do not hide behind our customs?"

"There is no reason to involve you in the white man's fight."

The Indian solemnly nodded. "It is *you* who shows wisdom. And courage. I wish you gentle winds and good hunting."

"Wish me strength to escape," said Slocum. "The men to whom you sold your land seek me. They go everywhere." He took out the papers he had stolen and spread them on the floor. They had become a little waterlogged but were still legible. "Do you have anything I can use to wrap these, to protect them from the rain?"

Buffalo Pizzle went to a small mound of his belongings and sorted through them. He silently handed Slocum an oilskin pouch bearing the U.S. Cavalry insignia. The Indian smiled. "From days when hunting was better for the Osage warrior."

Slocum tucked the papers inside, then stuffed the pouch

inside his shirt. He stood and left without saying anything more. The Indian had shown trust and even courage in allowing him to stop briefly. Slocum guessed that the Osage were not content with the way Kansas was being run and that they had no great love for Josiah Hammerschmidt. That didn't mean they would risk what little they had been given to right wrongs against homesteaders and drovers. They had problems of their own that might never be resolved.

Slocum swung into the saddle and rode on, heading to the south and west, hoping to avoid any posse riding out directly from Abilene.

He wasn't that lucky. He rode directly into a small band —and the huge man riding what looked like a massive Percheron pointed and yelled. Even at this distance, Slocum knew his luck had run out. The one man who could positively identify him as the thief in Hammerschmidt's office had crossed his trail.

Wheeling his chestnut horse due west, he rode for a small water-filled gully. He splashed through it and struggled up the far slope. From the top of the rise he counted his pursuers. Five. Too many to fight off, even if he had wanted to.

A break in the storm worked against him. The blinding, veiling curtains of rain had ceased and left a clearness to the air that made it hard to get away unseen. Slocum actually missed the rain—or even the dust storms which often ravaged Kansas in the early spring.

The land's flowing contours slowly went away and left Slocum riding on a flat plain offering no place to hide. He knew he stuck up as if he carried a brass flagpole with the Stars and Bars flapping in the wind. When the bullets began singing around him, he didn't worry much. Anyone shooting from this range had to be luckier than skillful. Even he would have difficulty hitting a moving target at several hundred yards. What worried him most was the lack of cover.

How could he outrun the five men? He had nowhere to hide on the flat prairie.

The sounds of horses behind him grew louder, more insistent. His steed valiantly tried to keep a steady pace, but the past weeks had taken a slow toll on her stamina. She weakened. His pursuers got ever closer.

Slocum looked around for a place to make his stand. There weren't even trees out here. The best he could find was low rabbit brush, which afforded no cover at all.

Bullets began winging past his head again. Those pursuing him didn't aim any better, but the slugs flew closer. They had cut down the distance considerably.

He rode bent low over his horse's neck. What worried him more than anything else was a slug hitting her. Left afoot on the prairie, he would be easy game for the men.

"Get him, you galoots!" cried the mountain of a man. "Hammerschmidt's offered a hundred-dollar reward!"

For that kind of money, these men would kill their own mothers.

Slocum cut at an angle to his direction of travel, hoping the small gullies cut by the runoff would slow the posse behind. It didn't. If anything, they got even closer.

A pair of large rocks—Slocum couldn't call them boulders—gave him his only hope of standing off the vigilantes.

He reined in and dismounted, dragging his Winchester from its scabbard. He levered in a round and fired, not caring if he hit anything. He had to stop the men's rapid advance or they would be over him in an instant—and that would spell his end.

They found the same problem now that he'd discovered already. The had no easy hiding place. They split up and began to circle. Slocum cursed. This was the best they could do. Keep him moving around, aiming at first one and then the other while someone rode down on him from behind. They were plainsmen; he was used to mountains, where a man could stand off an army, given the proper fortress from which to fight.

Slocum settled down and squeezed off a round. He heard a frightened cry. It sounded wrong for it to have been a clean hit. Not waiting, he swung to his right and fired again. A clean miss, but he drove the man back. Behind him he heard the rush of hooves. He fired twice more. This man he took out of the saddle. The impact he made and the way he lay unmoving convinced Slocum he had made a killing shot.

This didn't stop the other two on his left from attacking. He drove them away with four rounds.

Sweat poured off him. He had to reload. And the others moved in on him while he stuffed cartridges into the Winchester's magazine.

He got off another shot which stopped the huge man in his tracks—or so Slocum thought.

"Look'it that!" the man cried.

Slocum took the chance to squeeze off three more shots. When the posse didn't press him, he reloaded—and found he had only five rounds left for his rifle. With the six in his Colt, he didn't stand much chance against them if they kept coming for him.

To his surprise, they formed a small knot just out of rifle range and talked. He heard angry, frightened voices but couldn't make out the words. The four men remaining in the posse turned tail and rode like the wind back toward Abilene.

Slocum thought it might be a trick. He stood on one large rock and peered after them, trying to figure out what they were up to. He watched as all four vanished into the distance. The suddenness of their retreat took him completely by surprise.

He scratched his head. It didn't make sense. They had

him. One or two more might have got winged or even killed, but the lure of so much money from their boss should have driven them on. Even if they hadn't wanted to face him down, why not send a man back to town for reinforcements while the other three kept him pinned down?

Slocum sat down on the rock and shook his head. There was no telling what had spooked the men.

"Let's get on out of here, old girl," he said to his horse. For the first time, he looked due west—and saw what the posse had already seen.

Corroded copper green clouds scudded by just above the prairie. Giant swirls formed and lacy fine clouds dipped down.

From one storm cloud more than simple rain clouds trailed. The jumping, lurching power of a tornado had been unleashed on the Kansas prairie—and it was heading straight for him!

16

Slocum's horse reared and pawed at the air. Slocum felt like doing something too, but the helplessness that washed over him froze him solid in his tracks. The tornado danced and bobbed and came closer. When it was less than a mile away, the wind died to an eerie calm. Then a sound infinitely more frightening rose. He heard a deep thunder that shook the ground. It might have been a runaway locomotive for all the rumbling and crashing it caused.

He grabbed the reins and tried to hold the horse down. The bucking got worse. The horse's eyes showed the whites all around. Slocum knew the animal's fear and shared it. It was building up inside him until he wanted to scream and go running off across the prairie like a damned fool. That might relieve some strain, but what could he *really* do against the mightiest storm Nature could throw his way?

He slipped down behind the large rock, knowing it was a puny defense against the tornado roaring along the prairie, ripping up bushes and leaving behind a trail of death and destruction.

The wind picked back up and blew his hat off. He grabbed for it, but hanging on to the reins seemed more important. The horse tried to bolt and run; Slocum fought it to an uneasy quiet.

The green-bellied clouds arrowed by overhead. Along with them came the roaring funnel cloud. Vapor blacker than night spun with such fury that Slocum wondered if he wouldn't be sucked up even if passed by a mile away. He ducked behind the pitiful mound of boulders and held firmly to the horse's bridle.

Tiny bits of dirt and pebbles pelted him like miniature bullets. He put an arm up to protect his head. The roar from the windstorm got louder and louder until he knew he had turned deaf.

Then there was . . . nothing.

Startled, Slocum dared to peer over the rock. The tornado had lifted back into the green cloud. A swathe of ripped-up land marked where the tornado had briefly touched ground. Other than this, the potent storm might never have existed.

The horse tugged and jerked at the reins. He wondered why the animal didn't whinny and snort in protest. He saw nostrils flaring and teeth showing from behind equine lips and realized he *was* deaf. The intense roar from the tornado had left him without hearing.

But he still had his life.

Slocum walked the horse around almost thirty minutes before getting into the saddle. The animal balked like an old, cranky mule and then settled down. Within an hour, Slocum's ears alternately rang and buzzed. By sundown, he was able to hear again with his normal acuity.

For almost a week he camped out on the prairie, worrying over what to do. He thought of circling around and stopping by to see Claire but pushed that notion out of his head. She might have trouble with Hammerschmidt's henchmen—what had become of Trumble?—but they weren't likely to do much to her as long as he had the papers damning the railroad man. He patted the bulky oilskin pouch stuffed into his shirt to reassure himself that he hadn't lost it.

The packet gave him a nice, steadying feel. But in five days he had yet to figure out the best way of using the information against Hammerschmidt. They might have thought he'd died in the tornado or had ridden west and kept going. Either way would have been fine with Hammerschmidt. His hired guns might even have lied and said they left him buried in an unmarked grave on the plains.

Whatever had happened, Slocum still had to settle scores with Trumble and Hammerschmidt.

As much as he hated to admit it, going to Marshal Lewis looked to be the only way to accomplish anything. On his own he could do little to bring Hammerschmidt to justice. The director of the Kansas Pacific Railroad was too rich and powerful. Left unchecked, he would gobble up the homesteaders' claims for nickels and dimes. He had already robbed Frank McKenzie of his herd and life—and this had been only a small venture.

Slocum touched his vest pocket where the double eagle rested. He was still owed damned near forty dollars in back wages, too. The money wasn't as much the issue as was the fairness.

Seven days after he had run from Abilene, John Slocum rode back into town. He didn't make his presence widely known, preferring to stay to back streets and alleys. He returned to the livery and found the stable boy still working hard at reading the Abilene *Chronicle*.

"You back, mister? The way you hightailed it out of

town last week, I didnt' figure you'd ever show your face around here again."

"Tend to my horse," he said, not wanting to discuss his business with the boy.

"Money in advance." The youth peered at him over the tip of the newspaper, suspicion in his eyes.

Slocum glanced at the front page of the paper and didn't see anything about his being a fugitive. He decided the boy was naturally distrustful. He couldn't much blame him for that. The last time he had ridden out had been under mighty strange circumstances.

"All I've got is a twenty-dollar gold piece, but I'm going over to see Marshal Lewis. Come along, if you like."

"I'll look after your horse. Just don't go leavin' me to sell it to pay your bill."

"I won't," Slocum said, patting his horse's neck. "She's been too good to me these past months to abandon."

He went off in search of the marshal. He passed both the Longhorn and the Alamo. A quick glance into the latter saloon gave a glimpse of Doc Pendleton and another man sitting at the table in the center of the room. Slocum didn't recognize the man drinking with the doctor. Of Dykstra and Hammerschmidt he saw no trace.

Lem Washington sat on the hitching rail outside the marshal's office, long legs dangling, a quirly bathing his face in blue smoke.

"Didn't reckon we'd ever see your ugly face in these parts again," the deputy said between puffs. "You the one what caused the ruckus at Mr. Hammerschmidt's office?"

"Marshal Lewis inside?"

Washington bobbed his head up and down. "Reckon he wants to see you real bad. Can't say I ever saw a fugitive give himself up this easy, but then you're a danged hard one to figure out."

Slocum grinned crookedly and went into the marshal's office. Lewis looked up from a stack of papers he was leafing through. His hand drifted toward a six-shooter lying beside him on the desk.

"No need for that, Marshal. Take a look at these." Slocum tossed over the oilskin pouch.

"You been out palaverin' with Buffalo Pizzle, ain't you? I recognize his hand in this."

"The Indian's not been harboring a fugitive, if that's what you mean, Marshal. Look at what's inside."

"Now these wouldn't be the valuable doc-you-mints stolen from Kansas Enterprises, now would they?" Even as he spoke, he glanced quickly at each page. His eyebrows arched higher every time he turned a page. "This is right interesting."

"Makes a pillar of Abilene society out to be a first-rate crook," Slocum allowed.

"It does look that way. Seems Ralph Snodgrass is involved in forging land deeds up to his earlobes." Lewis said this with more satisfaction than Slocum would have thought.

"The land bought from the Osage is all legal and above-board," Slocum said, "but the forged land deeds might break federal law. That's all homestead land."

"Don't know that the Indians have the right to sell off their land, now that I think on it," said Lewis, rocking back in his chair and fixing his steely gaze on Slocum. "That's not really theirs. It's all government land, being a reservation and all."

Slocum shrugged. He hadn't considered that. He had been too intent on Hammerschmidt's other treachery. "There's something else, Marshal." Slocum went on to tell what he knew of McKenzie's death and how Hammerschmidt had bought the herd for a fraction of its value.

He finished, saying, "You can telegraph and find out if the beeves *were* destroyed."

The marshal frowned and shook his head. "That's all legal. I been followin' this closer than you might think. Can't blame a man for doing a slick business deal." He rocked back in his chair and laced his long, gnarly fingers behind his head. "Killing the drover what brung the beeves north from Texas, now that's a different kettle of fish entirely. But you don't have a shred of proof that Hammerschmidt did it—or that Trumble helped out with the murder."

Slocum reluctantly agreed. "What are you going to do about this?" He tapped the papers on the marshal's desk.

"Surely does bring up questions about Josiah Hammerschmidt's honesty and fair dealing. I reckon the real problem lies in how you came to get these papers."

"Found them."

"Reckon that's possible. Maybe one of them sneaky Osage Indians broke into Hammerschmidt's office and took them. The description of the thief fits you better'n it does Buffalo Pizzle." The marshal's eyes never wavered as he tried to stare down Slocum.

Slocum's cold green eyes bored back. He wasn't giving in an inch. He dared not yield or he would be the one in the Abilene jail.

Marshal Lewis heaved himself to his feet. He scooped up his pistol and stuck it into his holster. "Let's go see how Mr. Hammerschmidt answers some of these charges. Reckon he has a right to say his piece before I arrest his ass and throw it in a cell."

Lewis smiled from ear to ear and clapped Slocum on the shoulder.

"Lem, go fetch Bruno. We're payin' a call on Hammerschmidt, and it ain't gonna be a friendly one." Slocum trailed behind the marshal and the two shotgun-toting deputies as they went to confront Josiah Hammerschmidt with evidence of his lawbreaking. Somehow, Slocum didn't think it would be an easy matter to arrest the wily railroad magnate—not as long as he had hired gunmen like Trumble doing his bidding.

17

Slocum hung back, letting Marshal Lewis and his deputies go into the office building. The few customers in the bank lobby looked nervous. The tellers were even more frightened. Slocum reckoned they had known for some time what Josiah Hammerschmidt had been doing. It had only been a matter of time before some of the dirty dealing came back to haunt the man—and involve them.

"Mr. Hammerschmidt up there?" Lewis asked, indicating the stairs leading to the second floor with his rifle.

The teller's head bobbed, and he made funny gurgling noises. He wiped his mouth and turned even paler.

Slocum swung around, hand flashing to the ebony handle of his Colt Navy. He drew and fired in one smooth, clean motion. The bullet caught the man in the center of the chest, driving him back through the door. The shotgun he carried discharged and sent buckshot through the bank.

One woman moaned and slumped to the floor. Slocum didn't bother checking to see if she had been injured. She might have just fainted.

He had to work to stay alive. Behind the man he'd just shot down stood Trumble. The red-haired gunman's expression flowed like putty in the hot sun. His cockiness changed to anger.

"You!" Trumble had eyes only for Slocum—and a six-shooter in his left hand filled with lead death. He began firing, not caring about Lewis or the two deputies.

"Stop it!" roared the marshal. Lewis ducked when another gunman fired from the top of the stairs.

Bruno grunted and doubled over. Lem Washington rushed to cover the fallen lawman.

"Damnit, forget him," flared Lewis. "We got to stop those owlhoots before they kill every damn one of us!"

Slocum hazarded a quick look around the door and saw three men at the top of the stairs. Of Trumble he saw nothing. He swore. The redheaded outlaw had turned tail and fled. Slocum didn't figure him to be the kind to make a stand when the law came after him.

Two quick shots momentarily drove back the men at the top of the stairs. Lewis and Slocum burst through the door and positioned themselves on either side of the stairs leading up to Hammerschmidt's office.

"You up there, Josiah?" called Lewis. "Let's talk this out peaceable-like. No need for more people getting killed."

"Marshal, the teller says he ain't there," came Lem's voice from the bank.

"A fine time to learn that," snorted Lewis. "We got to clean out that den of rattlesnakes or we'll never see 'em again."

"Trumble ran," said Slocum. "Let me go after him."

"You ain't a deputy. What can you do besides shoot him down?" Lewis paused for a moment, then laughed harshly.

"Hell, *I* can't do more'n that and I *am* the marshal. Go after him. Just don't let me hear you went and done anything too illegal."

Slocum glanced up the stairs and got off a quick shot to keep the men back, then ran down the hall and kicked open the door leading into the side street. He almost expected Trumble to be waiting in ambush for him. The street stretched empty in either direction. The only sign betraying that another had passed by was a deep heel print in the dirt slowly filling with water from a nearby mud puddle. Someone had run past not long ago. It had to be Trumble.

It had to be. Slocum wasn't about to lose the man now. The memory of what he had tried to do to Claire burned in his brain. And he owed the red-haired outlaw for much more than this.

Slocum brushed light fingers over the wound on the side of his head. Trumble hadn't pulled the trigger, but he had ordered the back-shooting. That was good enough for Slocum.

He raced to the livery, shouting for the stable boy. Only frightened horses greeted him. Slocum slowed his headlong rush and moved more carefully, straining every sense to find what had happened.

A small pair of boots poked out from one stall. The stable boy had been brutally pistol-whipped. His chest rose and fell fitfully. He clung to life by the thinnest thread possible. Slocum searched the stables. Trumble had already fled, taking a horse.

Slocum saddled his mount and rode out quickly. As he passed the general store with its half-dozen old men sitting out front whittling and discussing the strange goings-on over at the bank, he shouted, "The stable boy's been hurt. Trumble did it. Get a doctor for him—and get word to the marshal when you can."

The men looked up, weathered faces showing no emotion. Slocum got the reins into his left hand and began using them to speed his horse after Trumble. He could only guess which way the outlaw had run, but he had a notion that it would be toward the Osage lands. If Trumble could use the Indians to hold up legal pursuit for even a day he might be able to get away scot-free.

Occasional muddy patches of road showed a horse had passed by recently. Slocum reined back to a slower pace. The other horse was galloping full tilt. It would tire soon. Very soon.

The country didn't change much from the prairie flatness, but Slocum saw signs of growing hilliness. He rode to the top of a small rise and peered into the distance. He had guessed right. Not a mile away rode Trumble. He had tired out his horse and now had to walk the animal.

It would take an easy twenty minutes to overtake him.

Then it got harder. The first shot damned near took off Slocum's head; his ears began to ring from the report. He hunkered down and rode bent over his horse's neck. When the next shot came, Slocum slipped from the saddle and hit the ground running. He didn't want Trumble shooting his horse out from under him.

"It won't work this time, Trumble. You can't bushwhack me twice. Come out and let's do this right."

"I'm not afraid of you, Slocum! Goddamn, I'm gonna blow you head off!"

Slocum settled himself and felt a deadly calm fill him. He stepped out and waited. Trumble showed himself from behind a rock, rifle in hand. The man tossed it aside and stood, stance wide, left hand poised over the butt of his pistol.

"I'm gonna love seeing you kicking in the dust, Slocum. You been a thorn in my ass ever since you came into Abilene."

Slocum didn't answer. He watched Trumble closely, waiting for the telltale tensing of muscles. Trumble's gaze flickered. Slocum drew and fired—and missed.

Trumble worked frantically on the butt of his pistol. He

pulled out his six-shooter and fumbled. It had jammed.

The red-haired gunman threw his six-shooter down and stood, waiting for Slocum. With a sudden jerk, Trumble dived to one side and scooped up his rifle.

The report echoed across the flat Kansas prairie. Trumble stared at Slocum and the smoking pistol in his hand. Then the gray eyes closed as the pain became too great. He died without a sound.

Slocum knew his second shot had been on target: Trumble's heart. He had no need to check. He returned to his horse, content to let the buzzards have Trumble.

By the time he got back to town, Lewis and his deputy had the situation well in hand. Lem Washington was covering four gunmen with his shotgun. The way his finger stroked the double triggers, he wanted to cut them down where they stood.

"What about your other deputy?" Slocum asked as he dismounted.

"Bruno got hit in the head. With that thick skull of his, he'll be all right."

"What's wrong?"

"Little Sam, over at the stable. He died."

"So did Trumble," Slocum said. "That goes a ways toward settling the score."

"Not by much." Lewis spat into the street. "Still got to locate that good-for-nothing Hammerschmidt. He's behind this. I swear, I'd put the noose around his neck if I thought he'd set Trumble onto the boy. Everybody in Abilene loved that young'n."

"Where is Hammerschmidt?"

"These four say he's over at the Armada Hotel. I find that a bit suspicious, but I'm gonna check. Come with me?"

Slocum and the marshal walked slowly toward the imposing hotel at the end of the street. Slocum hardly believed that they'd find Hammerschmidt there waiting for

them. The railroad man would have hightailed it out of
Abilene at the first shot. There was no reason to stay behind when the law was hot after you.

Slocum stopped dead in his tracks and blinked, thinking
the hot Kansas sun was confusing him with mirages. Sitting in a fancy restaurant not ten feet away was the railroad
director.

"If that don't beat all," marveled Lewis. "This is gonna
be easier than I thought."

"Why didn't he—" Slocum bit off the speculation. The
way of finding out why the conniving robber hadn't left
town was to ask.

Hammerschmidt looked up from his meal, only a small
flicker of surprise showing on his face. "Afternoon, Marshal." Hammerschmidt scowled in Slocum's direction and
said nothing to him.

"You got a heap of explainin' to do, Josiah."

"How's that, Marshal?" Hammerschmidt gently patted
his lips with a linen napkin. Slocum blocked the waiter's
path. The look he gave the man sent him scuttling back
toward the kitchen.

"Really, sir. I was about to order dessert."

"You know anything about swindlin' these sodbusters
out of their land?" Lewis pulled out the oilskin pouch with
the documents in it.

"I have many dealings. Not everyone considers them
ethical, though all, I assure you, are legal. My lawyer sees
to that."

"You mean he sees to the forgeries?" asked Slocum.

"Prove it."

"Reckon we're gonna try," spoke up Lewis. "From
these papers, it looks as if you're in hot water up to your
fat ears."

"I doubt that. I am a very powerful man."

"You were trying to buy the land to put in fattening pens
and a rail spur to get the beeves to market."

"My plans are extensive," Hammerschmidt said. "You'll have to speak to Mr. Snodgrass about these dealings. I seldom bother with the tedious details."

"Or what you tell your men to do? You tried to run the settlers off their land."

"Sir," Hammerschmidt said, his pig-eyes fixed on Slocum, "you are abusive, and I will not stand for it. If my employees become a little . . . eager in the discharge of their duties, this is hardly my fault."

"Trumble told me everything. About the Osage. About the thefts from the Kansas Pacific. About lots more."

Hammerschmidt's facade cracked. Blood rose and turned his face florid. With a bull roar, he shot to his feet and overturned the table, sending food and fine cutlery dancing along the wood parquet floor. He fumbled in a vest pocket.

Slocum reacted faster than Lewis to his unexpected attack. He got his pistol out and sent it swinging hard at the man. He landed the steel barrel on the side of Hammerschmidt's wrist. The railroad magnate let out a yelp and jerked his injured hand back. A double-barreled .44 derringer tumbled to the floor.

He bent to retrieve it. This time Lewis got his turn at the man. He swung as hard as he could and landed his rock-hard fist in Hammerschmidt's belly. The air gushed from him, and Hammerschmidt collapsed, weakly gagging.

"You surely did get a bunch from Trumble before he died," Lewis said, looking at Slocum.

"Didn't get anything from him. Just guessed. Gives you a place to start looking. Unless I miss my guess, Hammerschmidt's involved in a whole raft of illegal dealings."

"That lawyer of his might be a good place to start asking," said Lewis. "Never seen one of them that wouldn't sing all day and all night, too, just to keep his own hide in one piece. Ralph's got a lot of singing to do to keep out of the Detroit penitentiary." Lewis heaved Hammerschmidt to his feet and guided him toward the door. "You come along too. We got things to talk about."

This suited Slocum fine. He wanted to get some money out of Hammerschmidt for the herd he'd stolen off Frank McKenzie.

Josiah Hammerschmidt had a *lot* to answer for.

18

Slocum waited impatiently while Marshal Lewis and three others interrogated Josiah Hammerschmidt's lawyer. When the marshal came out of the small jail room just off the main office shaking his head, Slocum went cold inside. He knew what was going to be said long before the words came from the man's lips.

"He's a slimy bastard," said Lewis.

"Which one? The lawyer or Hammerschmidt?"

"Don't make much difference. Both of 'em. Only thing lower than lawyers are child molesters. Can't say where I put railroad directors in that." The marshal sank into his creaking wood chair, hiked his feet to his desk, and tipped back his Stetson. "Ralph's been singing like a bird, and not much of it does us any good."

"Hammerschmidt's going to walk away from all this, isn't he?"

"Didn't say that. Just won't be able to get him for all his crimes."

"Which ones?"

"Forget about cheating the Indians in a land swindle. We looked into that real good. The government owns the Indian land and is getting ready to ship the Osages south to a new reservation."

"So Buffalo Pizzle didn't have any legal right selling the land to Hammerschmidt?"

"Something like that. If anyone's guilty of a crime, the Indian might be it." Lewis chuckled. He laced his fingers behind his head as he appreciated the irony of the crime. "Bet Hammerschmidt thought he was gettin' the best of that deal, too. I figure to let the Indians keep what they made off him. Seems fittin' to me."

"What about the farmers?"

"The settlers' deeds are all taken care of. We got them refiled and all the forgery corrected. Don't reckon anyone's gonna complain too loud about it since most didn't even know it was happening. Hammerschmidt was just getting that part of his scheme going. That raises the question of whether a crime was even done or not, leastways in all the cases."

Slocum heaved a sigh. Claire's land was again hers—or as much as homestead land could belong to a woman. She had to maintain Benjamin Carson's claim to keep it, but Slocum didn't think that would be much trouble. Compared with what she'd been through, this would be easy.

"There's one thing that's real bad, though, from your side of the fence," said Lewis, looking squarely at Slocum. "We can't prove a damned thing about him rookin' your Mr. McKenzie out of the herd. Can't rightly prove much in his death, either."

Slocum nodded. He reckoned Trumble had been responsible—but it had been on Hammerschmidt's orders. Proving any such allegation now that Trumble was buzzard meat was impossible. Slocum didn't mind that over-much. Justice had been served, and Trumble had paid for all he'd done. Hanging might have been too good for him.

"What about the money from the herd?"

"Can't show that Hammerschmidt *didn't* destroy the beeves. No records were kept, and nobody's talking. Everyone's busy covering their own ass in this. Hammerschmidt still throws a lot of weight around in these parts, in jail or out. Money does that, you know."

Slocum closed his eyes and tried to keep calm. McKenzie's herd was gone, the money tucked away in Hammerschmidt's bank account in St. Louis or Chicago or even in New York. Slocum didn't owe a damned thing to McKenzie's worthless heirs, but he did want to get some of the money due him for working the drive. Any chance of that evaporated.

"The best he'll stand trial for is attempted land fraud?"

"Might be worse for him than that," said Lewis, smiling. "Seems there was a strange occurrence during the break-in at his office. A bundle of papers showing how he, Dykstra, and Doc Pendleton were in cahoots and swindling Joe McCoy got mailed by accident. Hammerschmidt's clerk found this fat envelope in the rubble after the break-in and saw it was addressed to McCoy, so he mailed it right and proper."

"You mean McCoy will be after his hide?"

"Already is. You don't need a telegraph to hear the screams all the way from New York. Joe McCoy's not a man to cross. Heard tell Hammerschmidt's already in trouble with the Kansas Pacific Railroad because of Joe's agitating. Won't stop there, either, mark my words."

Slocum took cold comfort in knowing that the powerful cattle baron was stripping the railroad magnate of his wealth and power. Josiah Hammerschmidt deserved far worse punishment for his crimes.

"You need me any longer, Marshal?"

"Don't go lookin' for trouble, Slocum."

"What am I going to do? You've got Hammerschmidt in jail."

"Maybe not for long. Bail's not impossible to raise for a man with his resources. His crimes don't really amount to a hill of black beans."

Slocum shook his head tiredly. He had been through too much and had gotten back too little. Tornadoes and gun-fights and getting drygulched had taken its toll on his stamina. His head ached, and he needed the kind of comforting Claire Carson could give him. It had been over a week since he'd seen her. He had ridden out with only a brief note telling where he was headed. She must think the worst by now.

"I'll leave him to McCoy's tender mercy."

Marshal Lewis laughed at that. They both knew that the cattle baron had no mercy in him. By the time Hammerschmidt got free of the criminal charges, McCoy would be landing on him with both feet, spurs jangling and heels a-kicking. It wasn't as much as he deserved, Slocum reflected, but it might be worse than gunning him down.

A man like Josiah Hammerschmidt needed the money and power. By the time he was driven out of Kansas, he would have neither.

"We can take care of Doc Pendleton and Dykstra, too."

"What's eating you, Marshal?"

"I'd hate like hell to come after you, Slocum. Can't rightly say which of us would end up the loser."

"It won't come to that. I'm thinking on settlin' down," Slocum said. The words startled him. He hadn't known he would say anything like that, but everything that had happened to him had convinced him it was time to put down roots. He had drifted too long, and he could do a lot worse than being with Claire and working the homestead claim until it was proved.

Lewis looked skeptical. He stood, dusted off his hat,

and spun, going into the inner room of the jail without another word. Slocum left, uncertain at first as he mounted and started to ride out of Abilene. The closer he got to the Carson homestead the more assured he became that he was doing the right thing.

He had seen and done things no man ever should. Riding with Quantrill not fifty miles from here had worn on him, physically and mentally. The bloody-handed killing had hardened him. With Claire he found an easier side, one he had denied ever since the war.

Farming was an unrelenting life, but it had satisfactions that he had forgotten. The smell of a spring morning, the feel of good earth running through his fingers, the satisfaction in knowing that his efforts brought forth wheat and corn and soybeans. He could run a few head of cattle. The Spanish fever wasn't the real threat the people in these parts thought. With a few chickens and a pig or two, that would give them all the food they'd need.

Slocum smiled at the notion of a few fruit trees. He missed fresh peach pie. Could Claire bake? He didn't know, but she could learn. She was smart and quick.

Just thinking about her and how they could build a life together caused a warmth to grow inside. He rode faster.

By late in the day, he trotted down the twin-rutted road leading to the sod house he remembered so well. Slocum reined in and paused when he saw a heavily loaded wagon beside the house. Four oxen had been put into the corral. Of Claire's horse he saw no trace.

He reached over and slipped the thong off the hammer of his Colt. Hammerschmidt and his cohorts were in jail and Trumble was dead, but that didn't mean there weren't other dangerous snakes slithering around on the prairie.

Riding to the house slowly, his green eyes swung around to take in every speck of cover. He wasn't going to be ambushed gain.

Slocum frowned. The wagon was partially unloaded.

Furniture had been stacked on the far side of the house, as if someone had come to stay. Small wooden boxes littered the yard, excelsior showing that the contents had been removed. There was no sign this had been done hurriedly, as if robbers had swept through or Indians had raided.

He pulled down the brim of his new hat to shield his eyes from the sun moving lower into the afternoon sky. When a burly blond man came out of the sod house, Slocum's hand dipped to his pistol. But he didn't draw. The man wasn't armed.

Stripped to the waist and sweating, the well-muscled man had obviously been working.

"Howdy, mister," the blond called. "Didn't hear you ride up. Climb on down and I'll get you some water."

Slocum silently dismounted.

"Don't see too many travelers in these parts." The man stared at him curiously. Slocum detected no fear or animosity.

"Where's Claire Carson?"

"Carson? You mean Claire Pelak? She's out back somewhere, tending to the chickens. You a friend of hers?"

"Don't remember seeing you before," Slocum said, avoiding the question. "You a relative?"

The blond man beamed. "Might say that. Claire and me's fixin' to get married soon as the preacher comes this way day after tomorrow."

Slocum leaned against the sod house, all strength gone from his legs.

"You all right, mister? You're a mite peaked."

"The sun. Heat's been fierce today. How long you know her?"

"Just got in a week back. Terrible storms across the prairie. I was looking for a place to hole up until the tornadoes passed by." The man offered Slocum a dipper of water. He drank slowly. "Lost my wife well nigh a year back down in Texas. Cholera, it was. Decided to come north and try my hand at farming here. Homesteading in Kansas is a sight easier than in Texas. More water around here, though it's hard to tell from this weather. Land's not been worked to stone, either."

"You stopped by and..." Slocum urged the man to keep talking.

"Not much to tell on that. Claire was needing someone to help out. This place is a mite run-down, but it has promise. I'm the best damn dirt farmer west of the Mississippi. Well, me and Claire hit it off real good." The man smiled even more broadly. "Never thought I'd find another woman to match my lost Emily. Just goes to show how wrong you can be."

"Reckon so," allowed Slocum.

"You want to stay for supper? We ain't got much. The crops ain't gonna be great this year, but next. Anyway, you're welcome to share what little we have."

"Mighty good of you," said Slocum. "Got a lot of miles to travel before I can rest."

"Where you headin', if you don't mind me asking?"

Slocum shrugged. "Doesn't much matter."

He swung up into the saddle and looked out over the land. There was real promise here. Turning toward the west, he started to ride off when he heard Claire's voice. He looked over his shoulder and saw her coming from the direction of the chicken coop. He considered what he should do, then waved friendly-like and put his spurs to his horse's flanks. The chestnut horse protested but gave a satisfying burst of speed to get him away from the farm.

Claire had needed a man. The blond farmer from Texas had come along at the right time. Slocum had been out on the prairie, doing what he could to protect her claim to the land and stay alive in the process, but she couldn't have known that. She couldn't have known he would ever return. He had left and been gone too long without letting her know where he was.

"John!" His name drifted on the still Kansas air. He didn't look back. He didn't dare.

Slocum kept riding until Claire and her new man were far out of sight. It took a lot longer before the hope she had promised him was out of his heart.